SHOE

THE BLUES &

EROTIC TO-DO'S

AN EROTIC COMEDY OF ERRORS

CHAPTER ONE

All Good Things Come to an End

Reader…he fucking dumped me!

Everything was going so well with Tom, after our recent erotic disasters we had been taking things really slowly and I was more than happy with that. As far as I was concerned I never wanted to see another pair of pink fluffy handcuffs again as long as I lived. As I predicted my cousin Adrian, firefighter and professional wind up artist, did not let it lie - he spent the whole of our Aunty Maureen's birthday party making subtle comments about me being tied up and searching for the key to happiness. Thank God I don't have to see him again until Christmas when he'll no doubt bring the whole thing up again and I'll have to deal with my Mum constantly asking what he's talking about. Anyway, enough of my dickhead cousin let's get back to Tom. We had spent the last few weeks going on lovely traditional dates, we held hands, cuddled and shared tender kisses. He had showered me with roses, chocolates and sweet little love notes, I was blissfully happy and content. He was definitely my Mr Romance and the time had come to see if he was also going to be my Mr Uninhibited.

I was so excited and my fanny was tingling at the thought of what Tom was going to do me. I'd bought yet more lingerie and was sure I'd be completely and utterly irresistible, my muff had been trimmed to within an inch of its life and I was ready to go. I cooked us a lovely meal, well when I say I cooked I mean I'd reheated some M&S ready meals and thrown away the packaging! The scene was well and truly set, we hadn't taken our eyes off each other whilst we were eating and I'd even managed to lick chocolate desert off my lips seductively. I decided to take the initiative and told him to grab a bottle of wine and a corkscrew and meet me in the bedroom. I lay on the bed trying to assume my most erotic pose, he took so long I must have tried every position in the Kama Sutra. Confused and a little concerned as to what had happened I went back to the kitchen. Tom was standing by the drawers corkscrew in one hand and the wax mould of Daniel's bellend in the other. I froze on the spot, he'd looked in the wrong fucking drawer, why oh why did I not hide my little souvenir somewhere less obvious?

'I found this in the drawer Ann, it's obviously not mine it's far too big'

The poor man looked mortified and had probably just developed a penis complex. I just stood there gasping air like a goldfish out of water. What the fuck was I supposed to say?

'It's okay Tom, I prefer a more modest penis...'

'It's not what it looks like Tom, it's just a left over from a sixth form art project I did...'

'I like to collect bellends...'

None of those worked and the last one sounded a little bit sinister. I was completely at a loss as to what to say, but in the end Tom did all the talking, 'I'm sorry Ann, I thought we might have had a future together but I really can't compete with this, it's clearly not going to work between us and I think we should call it a day.'

With that he smashed Daniel's bellend down on the work surface and left slamming the door behind him. So my future with Tom had been shattered along with my souvenir of Daniel which had been well and truly squashed. As I scraped blue wax off the work surface I felt totally bereft, tears streamed down my cheeks as I realised Tom could have been the one, my Mr Romance and Mr Uninhibited. I'd well and truly blown it.

It's been two days since Tom dumped me and I've decided I need to move on, fuck romance that shit clearly doesn't work for me. I can't sit around moping and thinking about what could have been, I need to look to the future, set my own agenda. I'm a strong independent woman…I don't need flowers or chocolates (well maybe occasionally). I need to go back to my original plan, no strings attached sex, Ann without an 'e' erotic goddess and mistress of my own destiny! I decide to start as I mean to go on and try out the bouncing love balls I'd bought but been too scared to try. Who needs a man anyway? I take myself off into the bathroom and the balls are clinking as I take them out of the box. I don't bother reading the instructions as it looks self-explanatory to me. I'll just pop them in, go for a walk and see what happens. I'm all done! It was all a bit of a faff putting them in, but one quick shove and I was sorted. I have to admit it does feel a little strange, I can feel them jiggling around as I move…I'm not sure, I feel like a fucking wind chime. I take myself off to the shop clinking and clanking as I go, every time someone looks at me I wonder if they know, they couldn't surely? I'm still waiting for my fanny to start tingling, but I think I'm far too self-conscious at the moment.

I'm sure the bloke I just walked past just gave me a knowing smile, maybe he can hear them? I take myself off home and decide to eat lots of chocolate and read some erotica...maybe that will do the trick.

So the chocolate and good smutty book have had no effect on me at all, I can feel a bit of weight up there but not much else, I try jumping up and down, hopping up the stairs and sitting on the washing machine during the spin cycle and...nothing! I think my poor foof is pining for what could have been with Tom. So that's that then, I think I'll just take them out and try them again when my vag is in a better place. I go into the bathroom to start operation love balls and realise I have no way to actually get them out, I have a rummage around and can't get to them, if anything I think I am pushing them further up. This can't be right, there must be a way to get them out. I'm trying to keep calm as I rummage through the bin to find the instructions, my stomach churns as I read them and realise that in my rush to pop them in I've also inserted the string which I needed to get them out! Fuckity, fuck, fuck, fuck with more fucks on top! Maybe if I stay standing up for a while gravity will bring them down. After pacing around for an hour and having another good rummage I ring around my friends, they all react the same way - hysterical laughter and then the suggestion that I go to A&E.

I can't see I have any other options, fucking hell have I not suffered enough the past few days without having to endure yet another humiliation?

I arrive at A&E and head down, walk slowly to the reception desk. It's fairly quiet and I'm sure everyone can hear me clinking with every step. I imagine them singing 'shame, shame, shame, shame on you' as I walk past them. Somebody just needs to ring a bell and the scene will be set! As I approach the desk my humiliation is complete as I see Little Miss Smug Bitch at reception, her eyes narrow as she sees me. She obviously recognises me, I've been here so many times I'm virtually family. I can't help but mumble as I try and explain what's happened...

'You'll have to speak up, I can't hear a word you are saying'

I explain again and her eyes narrow even more, her thin lips are twitching;

'You've come to A&E today because you inserted some...LOVE BALLS into your vagina and now you can't get them out'

Yes, yes and fucking yes! Why did she have to shout love balls? That was a touch sadistic in my opinion. My muff is clinking like a Newton's Cradle and my cheeks are burning with embarrassment as I sit down, safe in the knowledge that thanks to Little Miss Smug Bitch every fucker in the waiting room knows exactly why I am here. I find a seat as far away from anyone else as I can find and bury my head in a magazine.

It's not long before I'm called, the nurse shows me through to a cubicle. I explain yet again what I've done as she goes off to find a Doctor. Whilst I'm waiting it gives me time to think about my disastrous dating history over the past few months: Daniel, Josh, Spencer, James and Tom. Where did it all go wrong? Daniel, he was just perfect. Josh, could have been a prospect but for his psycho bitch troll from hell Mother. Spencer, gorgeous and charming but should really stick to horses. James, married fucking shit with a monster penis and Tom, lovely, kind, sweet Tom. I'm just about to start tearing up when the curtain swishes open and it's him…Dr Gorgeous a vision in scrubs. I immediately get lost in his beautiful blue eyes and welcoming smile, he walks towards me and I'm almost trembling with anticipation. I can tell you know, if my fanny wasn't chiming it would definitely be tingling.

'Good to see you again, Ann. Now what have you done this time?'

OMG, he said 'good to see you', I don't know what to do with myself, was it just a polite 'good to see you' or is he actually pleased to see me? He looks through my notes and asks me to explain again what has happened, I can see his in his face that he is yet again desperately trying not to laugh. I run through the whole sorry tale again, his eyes are twinkling as describe how I got the balls in with one large shove completely ignoring the fact that the string needed to remain on the outside.

'Obviously we are going to have to get them out for you.'

I'm horrified, I mean I really would love him to have a rummage around in my fanny, but not like this!

'I'm going to have a chat with someone from gynaecology and they'll sort you out, just remember to read the instructions next time!'

With that he gave me another one of his lovely smiles and disappeared behind the curtain. Finally, my fanny forgets that it's chiming like a carriage clock and starts to tingle. I think the balls are actually starting to work as it's quite an intense tingle…I can't have an orgasm in here, it just wouldn't be right! Thankfully just before the tingling reaches the point of no return the gynaecologist arrives. I take off my underwear and assume the position. She switches on the light and points it at my nether regions, oh my goodness my muff is lit up like Christmas tree…it even comes with it's own shiny baubles. I cringe as I see the speculum in her hand, but I needn't have worried it's all over in a flash. The Doctor hands me the still clinking balls which by now feel rather warm and repeats Dr Gorgeous' warning to always read the instructions before inserting a foreign body into my vagina. By this stage I vow that I will never be inserting anything anywhere ever again…but I have to add that doesn't include cock. I thank the doctor, get dressed and scurry past Little Miss Smug Bitch as I leave. I make a vow to myself that I am never ever coming back here, even if it means I won't see Dr Gorgeous again which would be a shame.

When I get home I immediately pour myself a glass of Prosecco and have a cigarette to calm my nerves…I know it's bad for me, but come on I think after today I deserve one. Although I am still sad about Tom, I can't let it hold me back. I have a life to live and I'm not going to be defeated in my quest for sexual liberation. I've decided to give online dating another go and I've reinstated my profile. I just have to remember I'm not in this to get involved, look where it's got me when I've let my feelings get the better of me? I can be an erotic goddess, I really can, I just have to be a bit more careful and maybe not so clumsy! I'm not going to be a slave to my phone and switch off the notifications before I go to bed, if anyone is interested I'm sure they can wait until morning.

The first thing I do when I wake up is check my phone, there are three dick pics but that doesn't surprise me now...I'm hardened to them! But I do still wonder why men feel the need to send you a picture of their penis, let's face it they are fucking ugly things at the best of times so what do they think is going to happen when they send somebody they don't know a picture of their schlong? Seriously, do they think I'm going to swoon and drop my knickers at the sight of their cock? Dick pics aside, I have actually received a message...Stanley, he doesn't say how old he is, but he's sent a fabulous black and white picture of himself, he is very handsome and he has a bygone era look to him, how very enigmatic. He lists his hobbies as playing bowls, dancing and fishing...he sounds traditional and a little old fashioned, he could be just the tonic I need. He doesn't mention what he does for a living, which is a little strange. Maybe he has a boring job and doesn't want to put me off.

I've been exchanging messages with Stanley and he's so sweet and formal, I get the feeling he's a real gentleman and I'm pretty sure he would never have sent a dick pic. So I've decided to meet him, nothing ventured, nothing gained and all that. I'd say he has the potential to be my Mr Romance, but my Mr Uninhibited?...hmm...I can't wait to find out!

CHAPTER TWO

Stanley

I'm seeing Stanley tonight, he wants to meet in the car park of the Red Lion pub. The Red Lion is one of the quieter pubs in the area and it tends to have an older clientele, but at least we'll be able to chat properly and get to know each other better. I've decided to dress casually, jeans and a top which shows a decent amount of cleavage, I get the feeling Stanley is a proper gentleman who won't want to rush things. He can woo me as much as he wants as long as he realises that I'm after a shag, nothing more nothing less. Tom broke my heart and I'm not going to let that happen again. I'm in control now and the only feelings I care about are below the waist. I couldn't have a long term relationship with Stanley anyway, can you imagine?...Ann and Stan, we'd have the piss taken out of us everywhere we went.

I've just arrived at the pub and I'm waiting at the rear entrance in the car park. There's no sign of Stanley and he's already nearly ten minutes late. It's starting to rain and my freshly straightened hair isn't going to hold up much longer, if he's not here soon I'm going to be a walking frizz ball. Hang on, a car has just turned into the car park, fingers crossed it's him! It's parked up and my heart starts to beat faster with anticipation, he looked gorgeous on his picture and I can't wait to see the real thing. Shit, it's not him, it's a little old man shuffling towards me with a walking stick. Why is he heading my way...maybe he needs help with something? bless him. I'm always available to help a senior citizen.

'Hello Ann, you look beautiful this evening, just like your picture.'

What the fuck, how did he know my name?...then it hits me like a ten tonne truck, this is Stanley! His photograph was black and white because it was taken over forty years ago. Why didn't I guess? The formal language, his hobbies, I mean who under the age of 60 actually plays bowls? It all makes sense now, he didn't mention where he worked because he's retired! The devious fucker has stitched me up like a kipper, he's older than my Dad and my Dad has just turned seventy. I thought Stanley could be my Mr Uninhibited, I suddenly feel a bit sick. The things I imagined him doing to me, I feel like an OAP...Old Age Pervert! My brain starts to work overtime as I desperately try and think of a way out of this situation. Then I look at his little face and begin to feel guilty, he's probably on his own and lonely. Oh, fuck it! I decide to have a drink with him, bring a little happiness into his life.

'Good evening Stanley, you're looking very dapper tonight.'

He did look very smart, he was wearing a tweed jacket with a open necked shirt and corduroy trousers, just the sort of thing my Dad would wear. Stanley puts his arm through mine and we go into the pub. I look mortified and he looks like the cat that got the cream. I decide the best thing to do is grab a table and get Stanley sitting down as soon as possible as even with his walking stick he doesn't look too steady on his feet. I go to the bar and order a half pint of bitter for Stanley (he's definitely not a Stan) and a large gin and tonic for me, I get the feeling I'm going to need a few! I take the drinks back to the table and Stanley gives me an odd grin as he wipes his mouth after a sip of his bitter, I'd say it was a bit leery but he's probably just pleased to be out and about. I don't quite know what to talk about so I ask him about his family, he tells me was married to his soul mate Doreen for nearly fifty years. They had no children and when she died last year it meant he was all alone, he missed her so much he decided to try online dating just for a bit of company. I feel so sorry for him and touch his hand to offer some comfort...he does that odd grin again and I'm sure he's dribbling. It's slightly unnerving, but I'm not going to jump to any conclusions, maybe his false teeth are a bit loose.

As the evening wears on the conversation flows and I actually find Stanley quite entertaining. I'm enjoying listening to his tales of intrigue from the bowling club, who'd of thought Phyllis would have caught her Bob behind the bowling club toilets having his balls tickled by Norma the ticket lady? They sound outrageous and I accept Stanley's invitation to go to the bowling club and meet them all. There's obviously going to be no hot sex tonight but I think I might have found a new friend in Stanley and if I can help with his loneliness then everyone is a winner. As we are chatting away, I notice the pub doors swing open. Stanley notices it too and his eyes are popping out on stalks, the woman who has just walked in is absolutely stunning, ridiculously glamorous with the looks of a super model. I look at her in awe and wonder if her date for the evening is better than mine? I don't have to wait long to find out, he follows her striding purposely to the bar, his walk looks familiar and when he turns his head I realise to my absolute horror that it's Daniel!

Shit, shit, shit, what do I do? He can't see me, not like this, not with my geriatric date. Though why I'm even bothered I don't know, there's no way I can compete with Miss Fucking Perfection Personified. I put my head down and try and blend in with the wallpaper, but just as I'm trying to be inconspicuous Stanley squeezes my knee, I'm not expecting it and jump up knocking my drink over in the process. The noise of my glass hitting the table makes Daniel turn around and he's looking straight at me. He clearly recognises me as he winces and puts a hand protectively across his crotch. He nods and gives me a half smile, I nod back and resist the temptation to ask how his bellend is getting on. I look on green with fucking jealousy as he puts his arm around his date's waist, he could so easily have been mine! He should have been mine, I think I will regret lighting that scented candle for the rest of my life. In an attempt to escape Stanley's advances I go to the bar and get another drink, Daniel has disappeared and I can sense Stanley staring at me. His eyes are burning holes into my arse, this really doesn't feel right, surely he's too old for all this? I'll have one more drink and then get off home, I think I've done more than my bit for Age Concern today.

As I sit down Stanley knocks his glasses case on the floor, he's grinning again and I feel sure it wasn't an accident;

'Be a love Ann and pick my spectacles up for me, my back is feeling a bit stiff.'

As I bend over to pick the case up and can feel his eyes burning into my cleavage. Now I'm really convinced he knocked the case on the floor on purpose;

'Nice tits!'

He didn't really just say 'nice tits', did he? Now where have I heard that before…fucking hell, it's him, the 'nice tits' guy who sent me the dick pic with the bulbous bellend! Well now I know, It wasn't just bulbous it was fucking mummified! I put the case on the table and Stanley is not only leering at me, he's salivating, he's gone red in the face and is clearly over excited. I'm partly annoyed and partly worried for him, surely this much excitement can't be good for a man of his age? I thought he was such a sweet old man, well he had me fooled the dirty bastard. I stand up and I'm just about to tell him I need to leave when he looks at me, clutches his chest and falls to the floor. This evening just gets better and better!

'Help somebody please, think he's having a heart attack.'

The bar staff rush over and someone calls an ambulance. I don't know what to do, so I pat his hand and say 'there, there', it's the best I can think of given the circumstances. Even in the midst of a heart attack Stanley can't help himself, I think he takes me patting his hand as a come on. He heaves himself up with the last ounce of strength he has and tries to nuzzle his head into my chest. Thankfully a member of the bar staff sees him lurch forward and thinking he is panicking puts a hand on his shoulder and gently moves him back. Another one of the bar staff tells me to keep talking to him, I don't know what to say, how the fuck have I got myself into this situation? Seriously I am fucking cursed, I think I must have upset the big man upstairs because my entire life is a disaster. Stanley is conscious when the paramedics arrive, they run a few tests and confirm that he is most likely having a heart attack. He's asking for someone to find Doreen as the paramedics help him into a wheelchair, he keeps saying her name over and over and I start to feel sorry for him again. He's all strapped in and as he's being taken to the ambulance one of the bar staff shouts;

'Don't worry Stanley, we'll call your wife and let her know what's happened.'

Well that's just the icing on the cake he's got a wife and I've been lied to yet again. Not only is he a dirty old man but a lying, cheating one as well! I truly fucking despair in men I really do. They think about nothing except their cocks, even the old bulbous ones. I sit back down at the table to finish my drink, it may have been a shit evening but I'm damned if I'm going to let a perfectly good gin and tonic go to waste. I run over the events of the evening and come to the conclusion that I should give up and become a crazy cat lady…no that won't work I'm allergic to cats. Maybe dogs then, that's decided. I'm going to fuck men off and fill my house full of dogs.

I take the last swig of my drink and I'm just about to leave when to my surprise and absolute fucking delight, I see Daniel walking towards me. He's definitely heading in my direction and he's on his own! I plump up my boobs and flick my hair back off my face, I'll show him what he's missing! Suddenly a house full of dogs seems like a shit idea.

'Hi Ann, I'm so sorry to see what happened to your Dad, is there anything I can do? Do you need a lift to the hospital?'

My brain starts to work overtime, he thinks Stanley is my Dad not my date and he's offering to take me to the hospital, just me and Daniel, alone in his car...I couldn't, could I?

'Thanks Daniel, that would be really kind of you.'

I fucking did, oh come on it's far too good an opportunity to miss! I get into Daniel's car, it smells of his aftershave and I'm getting muff tingles. We sit in silence as he sets off and can't help myself, I have to ask...

'I know I've said it before, but I'm so sorry about what happened last time we met...how is your bellend?'

Shit, maybe that was a bit blunt.

'It's ancient history Ann, best left in the past.'

What does that mean, has he forgiven me? Is his bellend okay? I resolve to not mention it again, I'm just going to enjoy the few minutes I have in his company. It does feel a little awkward as we chat politely about the weather, bearing in mind the last time I saw him I was stark bollock naked (apart from my defective stockings). I am wondering what happened to Miss Fucking Perfection Personified, but don't want to ruin the moment so I don't ask. She was probably his sister or the cleaning lady. We arrive at the hospital and Daniel has been nothing but polite and charming;

'Do you want me to come in with you, you might need some moral support?'

He is just perfect, but no I fucking don't want him to come in with me to see my imaginary Dad. I decline politely and quickly write down my mobile number;

'That's very kind of you Daniel, but the rest of the family are on their way so I'll be fine. Here's my number again, call me anytime to find out how Dad is getting on.'

I wave at him from the hospital entrance and as soon as I'm sure he's gone I jump into a taxi. I feel wicked and I'm sure I'm going to hell, but eternal damnation will be worth it if I get another chance with Daniel!

I'm home and feeling quite pleased with myself, I managed to snatch victory from the jaws of defeat this evening. I've not only managed to spend time with Daniel again, he's now got my number. I look at my phone just in case Daniel has called already and I didn't hear the phone ring. No missed calls but someone has looked at my dating profile and left a message. What would this one be, serial adulterer, pensioner, spanking fan? Actually he looks quite nice, Andrew. He's thirty four, which is perfect. Works in marketing, so we'll have something to talk about and he enjoys long countryside walks...ooh he could be my Heathcliff.   I go to bed and although I'm excited about Andrew I can't stop thinking about Daniel. Would he call me? Would I ever get the chance to redeem myself? I drift off to sleep and wonder what tomorrow would bring.

CHAPTER THREE

Andrew

Today I'm meeting Andrew, we're going for a walk in the countryside and for a spot of lunch in a country pub…how very civilised! I'm really looking forward to it, I've spoken to him over the phone and I can confirm he doesn't sound a day over thirty four. I've gone through my usual routine, long hot bath, exfoliation and muff trim and now the only thing I need to think about is what the hell do I wear? I haven't got walking boots, so will trainers do…where the fuck are my trainers? Are jeans okay and do I need a big coat? This countryside business is actually a lot more complicated than I thought. I think I've tried on everything sensible that I own. I even tried a head scarf, but I can safely say the Princess Anne look does nothing for me, maybe because I don't have that regal extra 'e'. I've settled on jeans, a light jumper and I found my trainers at the back of the wardrobe. Andrew is picking me up in a couple of minutes so I quickly check my make-up, spray my perfectly straightened hair again and pray it doesn't rain.

I'm in the car and can't help staring at Andrew. He is gorgeous, even better than his photos! He has the most stunning green eyes and the cheekiest smile I think I have ever seen. Is my fanny tingling?...it most certainly is! It's going well so far, he's chatty and very flirtatious. I think I could be in here. We arrive in a little village not far from where I live, it's very pretty and I can see myself living somewhere like this, maybe with Andrew and a couple of beautiful green eyed children. I mentally give myself a kick, I'm not in this for the romance, not at all not one little bit. We park up and Andrew takes a picnic basket out of the boot of the car. Warning bells start to go off, this looks a bit too fucking familiar. I remember what happened the last time I had a picnic with a gorgeous man and all I can see is Sylvia snarling at me. Surely I couldn't be that unlucky twice? I try and put Sylvia out of my mind, I'm sure Andrew has a perfectly nice, rational Mother who absolutely does not interfere in his love life.

We seem to have been walking for ages and everything looks rather green. There's not an awful lot to see apart from the occasional sheep and the wind is starting to get up. It's all a bit Wuthering Heights and I suddenly feel every inch the romantic heroine. I stride ahead of Andrew trying to look sexy as the wind blows through my hair. I turn and glance at him giving him my best come hither look and just at the moment when I look my most seductive my foot hits a rock and I stumble face first. I put my hands out to break my fall and my left hand hits something warm and moist, I look across and can see straight away… it's a steaming pile of cow shit! Does nobody clean up after cows in the countryside, have they not heard of 'Bag it and Bin it'? Fuck, shit, bollocks the cow pat look is not sexy, not one little bit. Concerned, Andrew drops the picnic basket and runs over.

'Ann, are you ok? That was quite a nasty tumble, what have you landed in…oh dear.'

Oh dear. I'm sitting here covered in still warm cow poo and that's the best he can come up with? He turns around and starts walking back, are you fucking kidding me? He's leaving me here, in the wilderness…what if I get eaten by goats?

Thankfully I misjudged him, he wasn't leaving me at all. He was just going back to get the picnic basket in which he had packed a packet of wipes…gorgeous and well organised! He's very sweet and gently wipes my hand down, once it's clean he offers me his hand and helps me back to my feet. Only my pride is hurt but I'm going to have to work hard to re-establish my sexy, erotic goddess persona. Right now I just look like a clumsy fucker who thinks cows should wear nappies. It's not long before we reach the top of the hill where we are going to have our picnic. Andrew opens the basket and throws a rug onto the grass, it's all starting to feel familiar again and I wait for him to tell me the picnic was made by his Mother;

'I hope you enjoy the food Ann, I got a local caterer to put it together for us, they're supposed to be really good.'

Now I am impressed, he actually paid a caterer to make our lunch, how posh is that? We chat as we eat and the food is spectacular, prawns, couscous, satay chicken…I wonder if I should ask him if I can take some home with me, there's more than enough. I quickly decide against this idea, nothing could be less erotic than me asking him if he could do me a doggy bag. The sun has finally come out, feeling full and contented I lie back and enjoy the gentle heat on my face. I'm feeling drowsy and just as I'm dropping off to sleep I feel Andrew nuzzling into my ear, I can feel his hot breath on my cheek and whiskers are tickling me (which is strange as I could have sworn he was clean shaven). Pleased as punch and fanny tingling I turn to respond. I open my eyes expecting to see Andrew's lovely full lips but to my horror the only thing I can see is a big shiny snout, I scream in shock and horror…a cow is licking my ear…a fucking cow! Andrew who had also fallen asleep wakes up, sees the cow and bursts into hysterical laughter;

'It's just a cow Ann, it won't hurt you.'

It won't hurt me? It was sucking on my earlobe…I nearly got intimate with a cow! The cow is completely unfazed and wanders off, probably to leave another cow pat for me to fall into. Do cows really just wander around doing their own thing, should they not be on leads or something? I really don't think the countryside is for me, how is this romantic? I can barely hide my relief when we pack up the picnic and head back to the car, we're going to pop into a pub in the village and right now I could really do with a drink.

Sitting in the pub, glass of cold Prosecco in hand I feel much more in control. Apart from when he's telling anyone who'll listen about the cow incident, Andrew is great company. He's quite into the whole countryside thing, he tells me he enjoys the freedom of the outdoors, how being somewhere remote make him feel anonymous and at one with nature. I didn't expect him to be quite so deep, it's an attractive quality and I'm starting to like him even more.

He's also very tactile which is nice, he keeps putting his hand on my knee so it's looking pretty positive, there really is an attraction there and I'm excited to see how this evening is going to pan out. We carry on chatting about anything and everything and two glasses of Prosecco in I'm feeling very comfortable. I'm just about to go back to the bar when Andrew suggests we leave;

'How do fancy a drive Ann, I've got something I want to show you?'

Well that sounds a bit mysterious and I have no idea what it could be, it's getting dark so you can't exactly see much. I agree and within minutes we're driving again. We head out of the village and down a dark country lane, I'm starting to get an idea what he might be thinking about and I'm getting muff murmurs. He pulls off the lane into a secluded copse. Andrew turns off the car engine, undoes his seatbelt and kisses me. A long, lingering kiss which takes my breath away. This is it, I'm living my erotic dream. I have never had sex in a car before…I can't wait! He kisses me again and puts his hand underneath my jumper, he negotiates my bra and plays with nipple, my neck arches with excitement as he kisses it. He quickly moves on from my breasts and unbuttons my jeans. He slides his hands into my knickers and roughly plays with clit, I reach for his dick but strangely he pushes my hand away. He's kissing me harder now and just as he senses I'm about to come he abruptly stops;

'That was just the starter Ann, are you ready for the main course?'

Am I ready? Too fucking right I am! Andrew starts the car again and we drive a short distance through the copse. I can see headlights in the distance and wonder if someone else has had the same idea as us. Andrew stops just short of the cars in front of us, he gets out and opens my door (gorgeous, horny and a gentleman). As he helps me out of the car he hands me a mask, it's a cat mask and I'm feeling a bit confused;

'Put this on Ann, it makes it more exciting when they can't see your face.'

They? Erm, who the fuck are they? Surely he means 'when I can't see your face'. Andrew has now put on a fox mask, so we are a cat and a fox...what the hell is going on? It doesn't take me long to realise, as we approach the other parked cars I see what looks like an arse pumping in the moonlight...my heart sinks when I realise it doesn't just look like an arse pumping in the moonlight, it is an arse pumping in the moonlight! Fuck me, they're brave shagging in the boot of their car when anyone could see. But its not just one arse, I count at least three in the back of different cars as well as various arms and legs hanging out of car windows, there's a group just watching and everyone is wearing a mask. There's so much cock on display I feel like I'm in a chicken coop. It takes me a few seconds to register what's going on and then it hits me...He's taken me dogging! Is this erotic, would I be living my erotic dream if I joined in...No I fucking wouldn't and knowing my luck I'd end up on Channel Four.

'I'm sorry Andrew, you must have made a mistake. This really isn't for me. I mean you wouldn't want to watch someone else have sex with me would you?'

'Damn right I would Ann, come on give it a try, you'll love it!'

The cheeky fucking bastard, he's seduced me all day, put me in grave danger from wild cows and now he thinks I'm going to shag a random stranger whilst he gets off on watching me. No wonder he didn't want me to touch his cock, he was saving himself for the shagfest he thought I was going to join in with. Well he can fuck right off! I tear of my mask and chuck it at his feet;

'No, Andrew, I won't give it a fucking try! You can keep your mask, keep your cows and keep your random dicks. Enjoy the rest of your evening but I'm off home.'

With that I head out of the copse relieved that I've had a lucky escape…I bet Heathcliff wouldn't have taken me dogging. Then it hits me. I'm out in the middle of nowhere, it's dark and I can hear cows mooing in the distance…do cows come out at night? I calm myself down and decide the best course of action is to follow the road back down to the village. I still can't believe it, what planet was Andrew on…planet fuck a stranger? What made him think I'd be up for dogging, was it the incident with the cow? Do I just give out dogging vibes, maybe I look like I'm into swinging as well? I'm muttering to myself all they way back which takes my mind off the fact I'm on my own wandering down a unlit country lane. It takes me nearly an hour to get back, I head straight to the pub, drink a glass of Prosecco in one and call myself a taxi home.

I'm home and have never been so relieved to be back in my little house. I resolve to never go to the countryside again. It's been a very strange experience and I'm never going to be able to unsee some of the things I've witnessed tonight. If dogging is what floats your boat then that's fine by me, but to be put into that situation without any warning was a bit of a shocker. To his credit, Andrew messaged me to apologise, he'd read the situation wrong and thought I was up for a bit of fun...yes a bit of fun with him, just him not with his countryside dogging crew. I don't care if he's sorry, he can fuck right off. He most likely sent the message whilst shagging the flamingo. I block him and remove all traces of him from my phone. I'm getting ready for bed when my phone pings with a message. I have to check just on the off chance it's Daniel. I would have thought he would have messaged me by now, if only to see how my imaginary Dad was. Unfortunately it's not him, but it's not all bad news. It's from Ethan, he's seen my profile and is messaging to get to know me a bit better. He looks really sweet, he's twenty eight, a bit younger than me and a mature student. Maybe I'll give him a go, I've never had a toy boy before. Think of all the things I could teach him: How to burn a bellend. How to avoid cheating bastards. How to get stuck in Handcuffs and lose love balls. How to steer clear of cows and mask sex in the countryside...the list is becoming fucking endless! My luck has to change at some point...doesn't it?

CHAPTER FOUR

Ethan

I'm meeting Ethan today. He seems fun, really down to earth and straight forward which makes a refreshing change. I'm waiting for him in town, we're going to a roller disco! It's non stop glamour for me at the moment...a fucking roller disco, what was I thinking? I haven't put on a pair of roller boots since I was ten years old and even then I wasn't very good at roller skating. I lacked grace, co-ordination and pink laces, a fact the other girls didn't let me forget. Thankfully even at that age I thought 'bollocks to them' I might not have been able to pirouette in roller boots but I was a genius on my Game Boy. I always preferred the company of boys when I was growing up, they were less complicated then the girls. I relished climbing trees and making mud pies...then puberty kicked in and they dropped me like a hot brick, preferring to hang out with the cool girls who had breasts and actually wore bras. I was a late developer and wore a vest until I was 15...oh, the humiliation when we got changed for PE. Thankfully by the time I got to sixth form I'd developed a bit of shape and the fuckers who used to hang on Julie Rigby's every word because they'd heard she gave her last boyfriend a blow job, suddenly became interested. I had standards back then and would never have considered Julie Rigby's sloppy seconds...I didn't know where their fingers had been!

I can see Ethan approaching in the distance, he's a lot smaller than in his photograph. He's quite slight, with sharp mousey features and he looks like a typical student dressed in jeans, baggy t-shirt and Converse pumps, he definitely has that 'pint of Guinness and a quick shag' look to him and if that wasn't bad enough, I am going to look like a fucking giant standing next to him. It's going to be David and Goliath all over again. Shit, shit, shit...I think I need to find a way out of this, I look for an alley way to dart down but it's too late, he's seen me;

'Hey Ann, great to meet you!'

He kisses me on the cheek and gives me a flirtatious smile, it doesn't give me any muff tingles, but it is quite endearing. He's so enthusiastic, like an excitable little puppy. There isn't an instant attraction like with some of the others, but he's kind of cute in a geeky sort of way...maybe he has hidden depths? Taking things more slowly is a good thing for me at the moment, I tend to get so carried away and then hit with crushing disappointment.

Ethan bounces ahead of me bounding up the steps of the building two at a time. I don't know whether to follow him or put him on a lead. We head in and I can hear music booming out of the rink, classic 1980's tunes…maybe this is going to be fun after all. We put on our roller boots and Ethan helps me to my feet (bless him, pulling me up must have taken every ounce of strength he had). He's really confident in his boots, I am impressed! He very sweetly holds my hand, I don't think it's because he's interested, I think he can sense I'm going to go arse over tit at any moment. We start off slowly and very wobbly, he holds on to me until he can feel I'm becoming more confident then he lets go and speeds around the rink, he's skating forwards, then backwards, he does a few fancy twirls and I must say there is something quite attractive about it. Despite my initial reluctance, I'm actually enjoying myself. After a bit of practise, I manage to pick the pace up to a bit of Wham, sing along to Whitney and almost moonwalk to Michael Jackson…however this was less skill and more trying to maintain my balance when starting to fall backwards and now somehow we are holding hands again and skating around the rink together. It's actually quite romantic and I must say I've impressed myself, I haven't fallen over once…I can actually roller skate!

Ethan smiles and makes eye contact as we skate, my imagination starts to run away with me. I imagine us alone and naked on the rink, he stands on his tip toes and kisses me masterfully. Taking control, he picks me up in his arms and I wrap my legs around his waist as he fucks me whilst skating (I'm not sure if this is actually physically possible but it's a nice fantasy whilst it lasts). Just as my fanny starts to tingle, reality hits. There's no way he'd be able to pick me up, he'd be flat on his back as soon as he tried and not in a good way!

We finish skating and go for a coffee and cake. I'm really starting to warm to Ethan. He's not classically good looking but his warm, funny personality more than makes up for it. He's flirtatious and has a naughty glint in his eye. I'm starting to think I could be in the market for a pocket sized boyfriend. I feel a pang of disappointment when he says he has to go. I really don't want today to end and it seems it's not going to;

'Are you busy tonight Ann, I thought we could try out the new Chinese on the high street.'

Am I busy, let me think…nope! I try not to look too keen as I accept his invitation. He kisses me on the lips as he leaves and I resist the temptation to pat him on the head. We really got on well today and I can't wait to see him again.

Although I've not got that long to get ready and I get the feeling I'm going to have to be at my erotic best!

I'm meeting Ethan in half an hour and I'm nowhere near ready! I've had a soak in the bath and I'm as usual I'm buffed and exfoliated to the point my skin is actually glowing. I don't know how I did it but got water in my ear and I just cannot get it to come out. I've turned my head to the side, patted my ear, held my nose a blown out of my mouth and it won't budge. I need to do my hair and get dressed so I'm going to have to hope it pops before I go otherwise I'm going to have to put up with muffled deep sea hearing all night. I've decided on purple lingerie tonight, I don't know why but Ethan seems like a purple kind of guy, he's a little bit different so I think purple will thrill him more than traditional red or black. I'm wearing a floaty, flowery dress which shows a little bit of cleavage and quite a lot of leg, it's the right balance of feminine and sexy as hell. I'll have to wear flat shoes as I'd tower over him in heels. There's not a lot I can do about my monster arse, but I get the feeling he'll thoroughly appreciate it. Just as I'm about to leave I get a message, it's from Stanley. He's out of hospital and recovering at home, he's wondering if we meet up again when he's better...erm no Stanley not only are you old enough to be my Father, you also have a wife. I really want to tell the philandering fucker to piss off, but bearing in mind he's just come out of hospital, I let him down gently and tell him that although I really enjoyed our evening out, I'm now in a relationship (hopefully).

We're in the restaurant, it's packed and my ear is driving me mad. I can barely hear anything above the noise in the restaurant and I keep having to lean right over to Ethan whenever he speaks…I suppose its not all bad news, he gets an eyeful of my tits each time and I can tell by the look on his face he can't wait to get his hands on them! We're onto our main course and he's getting really tactile, a stroke of the hand here, a touch of the leg there. We're chatting about our past partners (he seems to have had about as much luck as I have), when he leans over and starts to talk quietly, he looks around to make sure no one is listening which I find a little strange. I have to really concentrate on what he is saying as a party has just arrived in the restaurant, they have been seated at the table next to us and the noise levels are making it almost impossible for me to hear;

'You know what Ann? I'd love to bash your back doors in, how do you feel about a nice bit of rear entry?'

' That's very sweet of you Ethan, but you don't need to worry. I locked my back door before I came out.' He looks confused and starts to blush.

'No, what I mean is, how do you feel about…you know…fudge packing?'

'I thought I told you, I work in marketing. Nothing to do with fudge at all. Although I did help on a marketing campaign for some once.' I'm sure I told him what I did for a living, he's obviously feeling so horny he's getting confused.

'What I mean is, have you ever travelled the Hershey Highway?' He's starting to look flushed and irritable now.

'Oh, no I much prefer Cadbury, you can't beat a bit of fruit and nut.' I have no idea what I'm saying to offend him but he looks ready to burst.

'Oh come on Ann, you must know what I mean…have you got your brown wings?' His face has turned so red he's less mouse more tomato.

'I'm sorry Ethan, I can't hear you…have I got wings? No, I ordered the pork balls.' He's shaking his head and I think he's tutting.

'I'll try one last time, how do you fancy a spot of uphill gardening?' I can't quite make out what he's saying, something about my garden I think, but he's saying it through gritted teeth.

'I love gardening', his face lifts 'but I don't get much chance as I've only got a patio.'

With that, Ethan stands up and shouts so loudly even I can hear him;

'For Fucks sake Ann, do you take it up the arse?'

My ear pops and I feel water trickle down my neck. Just as I can hear again, the restaurant momentarily falls silent until the party next to us start to piss themselves laughing. I don't know where to put myself and Ethan looks absolutely mortified, he mumbles an apology and looks so crushed I tell him not to worry. It could have happened to anyone. Yep, most people end up shouting about anal sex in the middle of a packed restaurant at least once in their life…what a disaster! We quickly finish the rest of our meal in silence. I don't know what to say and Ethan clearly just wants to leave.

We pay the bill and do the walk of shame through the packed restaurant, I'm convinced everyone is looking at me and sniggering and I'm sure I just saw one of my old primary school teachers shaking her head. I try and crack a couple of jokes about me being deaf and him thinking I was taking the piss but Ethan just cannot see the funny side and doesn't even wait to find out whether or not I would have let him bash my back doors in;

'It was great to have met you Ann, but I don't think you and me would work. You would make a great friend and I'll send you a friend request on Facebook but I don't think we'd be right together in a relationship.'

With that he jumped into a taxi and drove off into the night. Who the fuck does he think he is?…I'd make a great friend, but I'm not right for him in any other way. Well he can shove his friend request up his arse, I was doing him the favour the ungrateful twat.

Another monumental balls up and I've come home alone…again. I think I need to contact some of the major TV Channels, I've got a great idea for a new series…'Dating Disasters'. I've got so much material it could run for months! I decide not to get disheartened, I am Ann without the 'e', a sexy, independent woman and I will fulfil my erotic fantasies. It's quite clear to me, I just haven't met the right man yet and just as I'm wondering what exactly the right man is my phone rings. Oh my goodness…it's Daniel! I take a breath and compose myself before answering;

'Hola'

'Hola' now that's right up there with 'Yoo Hoo'. What the fuck, I was trying to stay composed, I should have purred a greeting in low sexy whisper. But no, I channelled my inner Benidorm and now the moment might be lost;

'Hi Ann, sorry I didn't call sooner. How's your Dad getting on?'

I'm so delighted to hear his lovely voice for a split second I forget I'd made up an imaginary Dad to hide the fact I'd gone on a date with a septuagenarian;

'My Dad's absolutely fine, why?' Shit!

'Erm, because the last time I saw you he'd just had a heart attack.' He sounds a little suspicious, so thinking on my feet I manage to pull it out of the bag;

'Sorry Daniel, I've blocked it out it was so traumatic. He's doing well, making a great recovery.'

He doesn't suspect a thing, I really am going to hell aren't I? The rest of the phone call was lovely, Daniel was so concerned for me and I played my part perfectly…so perfectly he asked me if I would like to go out for a meal. It took me all of about a second to agree! I am so excited, I've got a second chance with Daniel, my Mr Romance and Mr Uninhibited all rolled into one. It's going to be perfect and I am going to give him the time of his life…once fucked never forgotten, that's me. I just need to remember to hide all the candles!

CHAPTER FIVE

Daniel Part Two

I'm meeting the delectable Daniel tonight and I am beyond excited. We're meeting at the Petit Restaurant again (thank goodness I've got a sympathetic bank manager) and if I'm going to be mingling with a load of posh birds everything has to be perfect. I've already had my hair done and now I'm waiting to get my bikini line waxed. As you already know I have an allergy to hair removal cream and after developing muff balls I decided the best approach was to go au naturale. I've been trimming and trying to tame my unruly bush the best I can, but now I think I need to leave it to the experts. I get called into the consultation room and take a seat;

'Hi Ann, so what am I doing for you today?'

' I don't want a Brazilian, I just want to go with the plainest option.' I can't remember what the wax I want is called, but I know it's definitely not a Brazilian...far to exotic.

'OK, so were going for a Hollywood then?'

I haven't got a clue what a Hollywood is, but if it's not a Brazilian it must be the one I'm thinking about. She asks me to take off my knickers and jump onto the bed…it's been a long time since anyone told me to do that! I do feel a little embarrassed but console myself in the fact that the poor woman is probably looking at fannies all day long, and once you've seen one, you've seen them all. She asks me to lift one of my legs to the side, and confusion immediately sets in. I've never had this done before and I'm sure she knows what she's doing. She reaches for the hot wax and before I know it my left fanny flap feels warm…no, this is wrong. I didn't want my flaps done…when I said plain, I meant plain as in just an ordinary wax, not plain as in take everything off and leave me bare. Before I can open my mouth she pops on the strip and….rip! I'm so shocked I scream at the top of my voice;

'Fucking hell fire, what the fuck was that!'

I think everyone in the beauty parlour must have heard as one of the other beauty therapists flies into the room and asks if everything is all right. I explain, that everything is fine. I've never had an intimate wax before and it was a bit of a shock. I didn't want to admit that I didn't have a fucking clue what I had consented to. Much as I didn't want to, I had to carry on. I couldn't meet Daniel with one bare flap, that would be ridiculous. I brace myself for the inevitable pain as the therapist continues my de-bushing and feel nothing but relief as she finishes and applies wonderful cooling body lotion to my now bare nether regions. I look down and my muff looks like a raw chicken, lets hope Daniel likes it enough to stuff it! As I leave the beauty parlour and start to walk home I feel strangely liberated...no hair, don't care! I've had a Hollywood, I'm now every inch an erotic goddess. I can finally cross something off my list of erotic ideals...I know I said let your muff be, but this feels great and you can't accuse me of abandoning my principles as it did happen by accident rather than design. When I get home, I can't resist having another look, it's a bit red but I'm sure that will calm down before I meet Daniel. I've got a bit of time to kill do I decide to read some erotica before I get ready...or should I call it some last minute revision.

I put on a final coat of red lipstick and even if I do say so myself, I look hot. I've opted for a classic little black dress with modest heels and no tights or stockings. I've been practising flicking my perfectly straightened hair out of my face coquettishly, I'm going to give Daniel the full performance tonight. I've got a sparkly new muff and I have every intention of using the new and unopened packet of condoms in my drawer. It's funny how things work out isn't it? If I hadn't of gone on the date with Stanley I wouldn't have bumped into Daniel and if Stanley hadn't of had a heart attack I wouldn't be here now waiting to go and meet my perfect mix of Mr Romance and Mr Uninhibited. I feel like the universe is smiling on me and my luck is finally changing.

Daniel is waiting for me when I arrive at the restaurant, he is as gorgeous as ever and my fanny is not just tingling but vibrating just at the sight of him;

'You look stunning Ann, it's so good to see you. I hope you don't mind, I bought you a little gift.'

Do I mind, not a bit! I open the black velvet box and it's a beautiful silver initial 'A' necklace. I think it's silver but it might even be white gold...I'll check when I get home, I can't really start looking for the hallmark whilst he watches can I? He takes it out of the box and I lift up my hair as he fastens it around my neck...this is so romantic, it's like something out of a film. Get in!!! He thinks I look stunning, he's pleased to see me and he's given me a necklace. I couldn't have asked for a better start to the evening. We enter the restaurant and are immediately greeted by Marcel the maitre d', he looks at me with a flicker of recognition…you better get used to me Marcel, I'm going to be a regular from now on. Daniel pulls out my chair and I sit down marvelling in his magnificence. He's incredibly attentive and still so concerned about my Dad. I play the part of the worried daughter to perfection (the Devil is taking notes) and he touches my hand gently, in his mind he's offering me comfort, in mine my fanny is calling out to him. He really is so fucking fit it's unbelievable, his expressive blue eyes, his smile…everything. He orders our food and I'm praying he orders the oysters again, not because I like them, they are fucking disgusting, but I want to watch him tease them with his tongue again and imagine it's me. The starter arrives and its smoked salmon mousse in puff pastry, damn I really wanted to watch him in action with the oysters! We chat about anything and everything and the champagne is flowing. There's one question I have to ask him;

'Daniel, when I saw you in the pub that night, who was that woman you were with?' Oh shit, have I just made myself look really needy, why can't I keep my fucking mouth shut!

'She was my date Ann, but she left early…she said I kept looking at you.'

I can hardly compose myself, he was staring at me not at Miss Fucking Perfection Personified. Staring at me, Ann without an 'e' she of the big arse and wobbly thighs. I can feel myself start to blush and I'm so excited I inhale the mouthful of salmon mousse I'd just started eating. I can feel it at the back of my nose and begin to cough and gasp, Daniel leaps up from his seat and starts to pat me hard on the back, my arms are flapping as I try to explain I'm not actually choking but he carries on until he's convinced I'm not going to die on him. He looks so worried and keeps asking me over and over again if I'm okay. Half the restaurant is watching and Marcel stands in front of the table with his arms outstretched so no one can see, this is just fucking typical but it could be worse, at least he's not talking about anal sex at the top of his voice. Panic over, Daniel sits back down and I take a huge gulp of champagne. Marcel is glaring at me, I'm clearly lowering the tone and I think I'm on my final warning!

We get to dessert with no more disasters and over coffee Daniel surprises me again;

'So, am I coming back to yours?'

I'm really struggling to maintain my composure and my mouth starts talking before my brain can censor what it's going to say;

'Too fucking right you are.' Do you think I'm coming across as too keen?

Daniel pays the bill...again and we jump into a taxi. We can't keep our hands off each other in the cab and I'm not sure how the driver managed to keep his eyes on the road. As we get out of the taxi Daniel picks me up in his arms and carries me to my front door, I scramble to get my keys out of my bag and we tumble into my hallway laughing...please somebody pinch me, is this really happening?

We are kissing as we walk down the hall, fuck the bedroom, I drag him into the kitchen (rule of erotica number 32, you always have to have a shag in the kitchen). He kisses me harder and with more urgency as he lifts me onto the work surface. Daniel pulls my dress down to expose my breasts and as he sucks on my nipples he slips his hands into my knickers and gently plays with me. I unzip his trousers and he is erect. As I run my hand up and down his shaft he groans as he slips his fingers inside me. By this point I am desperate for him, I whisper 'take me now Daniel' in his ear and he moves my knickers aside, I guide his cock towards me and just as he is about to go in…I wake up! What the fuck, you're telling me it was all just a dream? I quickly touch my neck, no necklace. Then I check my muff and it's got more bush than the Australian outback…it was just a beautiful, horny, unforgettable dream. I remember Daniel calling to check on my imaginary Dad, we weren't on the phone all that long but after speaking to him I felt so content I must have fallen asleep.   I get up and go into the garden to have a cigarette, I need one after the dream action I've just had. I'm starting to think that Daniel is nothing more than an unobtainable dream, he called me because he's polite, caring and perfect not because he fancies me. I need to move on and put Daniel to the back of my mind, although I wouldn't say no to another dream like the one I've just had…it was fabulous!

In the spirit of moving on I check my phone to see if there's been any action from the dating site and yes, as well as two equally horrendous dick pics, a lovely lady has very kindly sent me a picture of her vagina…how on earth do I respond to that?

'Thanks so much for the picture of your vagina, I was going to have a kebab for tea but I don't think I'll bother now.'

'I'd love to chat but I'll have to labia and leave you.'

'Is it winking at me?'

I think the best option is to say nothing, I don't want to offend anyone because at this point in my quest for sexual liberation I really need to stay open minded. Just as I delete the pictures my phone pings with a message, I cross my fingers and pray it's an actual message not random genitalia. Thank fuck for that…it's from Ryan. He's forty years old, an art teacher who lists his hobbies as rugby, football and painting. I wonder if he paints football matches? He doesn't look forty on his picture, which rings some alarm bells after the whole Stanley experience so I decide to go back to bed and sleep on it before I decide what to do. As I drift off to sleep I wonder what would have happened if my dream was real. Would I be snuggled up with Daniel now, my head lying on his muscular chest content in post-coital bliss? Could it have been the start of something more? How many bridesmaids would I have? So many questions, to which I had to finally accept I would never get the answers.

CHAPTER SIX

Ryan

I decide to leave it a couple of days before I contacted Ryan. I just needed to take a bit of time to completely get Daniel out of my system and I'm pleased to say I'm ready to move on and see where Ryan takes me. I'm meeting him later on today, we're going to the cinema which should be fun. I told Ryan to choose a film, so I've no idea what we are going to see. I bet it will be something intelligent and arty given that he's an art teacher. I'm dressing casually (I seem to be doing a lot of that lately) and have settled for jeans, shirt and my beloved cherry red DM's. As I look back on my recent dates I'm starting to long for a pint of Guinness and a quick shag, at least I was getting some sex even if it was a little dull. Now I'm having to content myself with regular Ann Summers deliveries, my local rep loves me...I'm her best customer!

I'm meeting Ryan in a café next to the cinema, he thought it would be a good idea to have a coffee first as we wouldn't be able to chat whilst we were watching the film.

My heart sinks when a frail old man enters the café...shit, have I been done over again? This one looks even older than Stanley. Just as I'm about to sneak out through the fire escape, I see a tanned, muscular arm reach out to hold the door open so the old man can get through with his walking frame. There standing before me is an absolute Adonis! Ryan is tall and extremely muscular. He has a strong, square jawline that makes him look like a super hero, I'd love to see him in a cape...just a cape! He recognises me from my photograph and waves. I stand up to greet him and he gives me a firm handshake...a bit formal, but never mind. He gets himself a cup of coffee and takes a seat opposite me. The conversation is a bit stilted at first, he actually comes across as a little shy. So I decide to take control;

'I haven't been to the cinema for ages, what are we going to see?'

That seems to do the trick as he starts to talk enthusiastically about the film we are going to see;

'I booked tickets for Death Knocks Twice - part seven, It's a brilliant series. I've loved them all and I can't wait to see this one. It's the final one and supposed to be the most gruesome, have you seen any of them?'

Well, that couldn't be further removed from an art house film could it? I don't quite know what to say, I haven't seen any of the previous films and I'm not a horror fan…I hate the sight of blood. I decided to be completely honest and tell Ryan I am a Death Knocks Twice virgin and ask him to give me a quick rundown of what the films are about…ten minutes later I wish I'd never asked. Basically Death has gone rogue and he's indiscriminately killing people, so if you are a twat and attract Death's attention he'll knock on your door twice and kill you when you answer. The franchise has been so successful they've stretched it to seven films, which in reality means this film is going to be shit. I try and look as enthusiastic as possible when if I'm honest, I'd rather watch paint dry. I won't even be able to sit and stare at Ryan because it will be fucking dark.

We take our seats in the cinema with a plentiful supply of popcorn, as the film starts Ryan pats me on the knee reassuringly I think he can tell I'm not 100% looking forward to it. It starts off innocently enough with the classic cheesy horror film teenage party. The party is in full swing with lots of alcohol and noise. One of the girls is being loud, obnoxious and a complete pain in the arse upsetting everyone with her mean girl persona…this doesn't bode well for her. She's sitting on her own now because she's pissed everyone off including her boyfriend, Brad, and no one wants to speak to her. Just as I predicted someone has just knocked on the door twice and arsey girl gets up to answer it...don't do it! She answers the door and is greeted by the sight of Death who looks menacing in his hooded black cloak, in his hand he is holding a large, shiny scythe. Arsey girl screams in horror and before she can close the door (and before I can cover my eyes) Death swings the scythe and...chops her head clean off. It hits the floor with thump, my stomach lurches and I jump out of my skin throwing a whole bucket of popcorn over the couple behind us. There's so much blood, I feel a bit nauseous and slightly light headed. I scramble out of my seat;

'Sorry Ryan, I need to pop out and get some fresh air.'

I try my best not to faint as I make my way outside, I knew this would happen. Why the fuck did I agree to go and see a horror film? As I take deep breaths of air, I hear footsteps behind me. I turn around and I'm thrilled to see it's Ryan. I had half expected him to stay in the cinema and finish the movie, but he is so lovely. He sits next to me and holds my hand...are those fanny tingles I can feel? He apologises profusely for choosing that film and refuses to go back in when I tell him it's fine if he wants to carry on watching;

'I just live around the corner Ann, do you want to go back to mine and I'll get you a brandy.'

I   t takes me a split second to agree and part of me hopes he'll be a real super hero and carry me home. We'd be like Lois Lane and Superman. Unfortunately I'm walking, but he carries on holding my hand. I could be onto something here and I need to get my erotic goddess head on, once my head stops swimming!

Ryan's flat is just as I imagined it would be, all arty and bohemian. I stare at the paintings and pencil drawings on the wall...they are all nudes and really quite beautiful;

'Did you do these Ryan, they are amazing.'

'Thanks Ann. Yes they are all mine, I love drawing the female form...would you like me to draw you?'

Would I what now? An absolutely stunning, charming, single man asking me if I want to get my kit off, what would you do?   I take a large sip of brandy and excitedly agree. Ryan shows me to his bedroom and tells me to undress and put on his dressing gown. As I get undressed I start to have second thoughts, are my tits pert enough? Will he be able to see my cellulite? Is my bush too unruly?...actually that's not too much of a worry considering how bohemian his flat is, he probably likes his fannies circa 1970. There's no turning back now, in for a penny in for a pound and all that! I get undressed and feel relieved Ryan hasn't seen my passion killing big yellow knickers and grey sports bra. When I'm ready I come out and he's waiting, pencil and paper in hand. He looks very serious and incredibly focused, he doesn't flinch when I take off the dressing gown and lie back on the settee. I feel like Kate Winslet in Titanic and I can't resist quoting her famous line;

'I want you to draw me like one of your French girls.'

Ryan looks at me blankly, he doesn't have a clue what I'm talking about. I explain about the scene in the film, he hasn't seen it so the reference is lost on him...how has he not seen Titanic! I move on quickly and try and adopt my most erotic pose, you really couldn't get more erotic goddess than this;

'Are you alright Ann, do you have cramp? You look a little awkward there.'

He gets up and poses me on the settee, his touch send an electric tingle through my body, there is definitely an attraction there, for me anyway. Ryan is being the consummate professional and is not at all fazed by my nakedness. I'm not sure whether he fancies me or not, he's not giving anything away.

Time passes very slowly when you are stark bollock naked and lying perfectly still on a gorgeous man's settee. It's actually quite boring trying to look erotic and it's the best I can do to stop myself falling asleep, thankfully the fear of dropping off and dribbling keeps me awake. After what seems like an eternity, Ryan tells me my drawing is finished. It's probably nowhere near finished, but I think me asking 'are you done yet?' every few minutes was getting on his nerves...I've been like an annoying child on a car journey and I think he's lost patience with me. I put the dressing gown back on and Ryan turns the paper around to show me...it is actually finished and it's beautiful and very flattering!

'I can't believe that's me!'

'Why not, you're a very beautiful woman Ann. Your lumps and bumps make you real.'

Lumps and fucking bumps, cheeky bastard! He did call me beautiful though so I'll let him off just this once. He tells me to go and get dressed and he'll get me another brandy. That's a bit disappointing, I was hoping he'd want to see a bit more of me naked! We sit fully clothed on the settee and Ryan tells me about his love of teaching, he really cares for his pupils and wants them all to achieve their potential…magnificent and dedicated! I nod knowingly when really I'm just concentrating oh his face, he looks so rugged but gentle at the same time. We chat for an age and just when I think he mustn't be interested in me, he pulls me towards him and kisses me. It's the most intense kiss I think I've ever had, he starts slowly, gently teasing my lips. Ryan holds me tighter as he kisses me harder, deeper and more intensely. I'm just about to reach for his dick when he jumps up;

'Shit Ann, I'm supposed to teaching an art class in ten minutes.'

Fuck, fuck, fuckity fuck! Every fucking time I get close, something happens! He keeps saying sorry as he ushers me out of the front door;

'I've really enjoyed today Ann, I'm so sorry I've got this class. I'll call you.'

Hmm, my suspicions are aroused so I decide to hang about for a couple of minutes just in case his 'wife' comes home. I've been here before with James so I'm sorry if I come across as not very trusting. I wait around the corner and there's no sign of anyone else going into the flat. I quickly check my phone for local art classes and it's there, Art for Beginners with Ryan Jones. He was telling the truth...you can't blame me for wondering considering the experiences I've had recently. I'm just about to head back home when Ryan comes out. I quickly fling myself over a hedge but I'm a split second too late and he sees me;

'Ann, is that you? Are you ok?'

Mortified, I drag myself up from behind the hedge covered in mud and pulling leaves out of my hair;

'Oh I'm fine, I dropped my mobile and as I reached over to grab it I fell. I've always been a bit clumsy.' I finish the sentence off with a girly laugh, I'm not sure whether I sound flirtatious or completely bat shit crazy?

'Just so long as you are ok, got to dash. I'll call you'.

As I wave Ryan off I feel renewed sense of optimism. I'm trying not to get over excited and have to remind myself yet again that I'm in this for a good hard shag and nothing more. Emotions are there to be messed with so I'm leaving them out of the equation...although I do have to say Ryan and me would make beautiful babies.

CHAPTER SEVEN

Doreen

I arrive home and I'm still on cloud nine after my afternoon with Ryan when Doreen calls. I don't recognise the number at all and break my rule of not answering numbers I don't know just in case it's Ryan calling me from a different phone;

'Hello, is that Ann? I think you know my husband Stanley.'

I'm completely taken aback and have not got a clue what I'm supposed to say. I immediately feel horrendously guilty, the poor woman. She's quite calm and doesn't kick off but she would like to meet me for a chat. What do I do? Tell her to fuck off and put the phone down, it's not my fault her husband is deceitful old bastard, or do I agree to meet her for coffee? I can't swear at an old lady so agree to meet her for coffee. She's already in town and the shops shut soon so we're meeting in half an hour. I'm starting to feel a little worried. What does she want, is she going to hit me with her handbag? Thankfully my conscience is clear, I had no idea

Stanley was married…I had no idea Stanley was a randy old goat. How the fuck do I get myself into these situations?

Doreen is already waiting for me when I arrive at the coffee shop. She doesn't look as old as Stanley, she's incredibly glamorous and has a youthful glow. I get myself a coffee and sit down;

'Thanks, so much for coming Ann, please don't worry I'm not angry at you. I just wanted to apologise for my wanker of a husband.'

I nearly spat my coffee out! She's clearly not happy with him and has no intention of chasing me down the street calling me a brazen hussy, relief sweeps over me as she tells me her story;

'I was very young when I met Stanley and, well, it was a bit of a whirlwind really. He was incredibly good looking and such a catch. I should have seen the warning signs, he was vain and flirtatious with other women when we went out...he described himself as having movie star looks and frequently told me how lucky I was to be with someone so good looking. Unfortunately I was blinded by love but it didn't take me too long to get the feeling he didn't think I was good enough for him. We quickly married and had two sons. It was when the boys were small I found out about his first affair and I don't mind saying it broke my heart, but my family loved him and persuaded me to give him another chance, it was just a mistake they said. I ignored the little voice in my head that was telling me to dump the bastard. Things were fine for a few years, but as I got older and my face became more lined he started looking for excitement elsewhere. It was always younger women, he was so arrogant. I think that's what he felt he deserved, a younger woman on his arm as a sign of his masculinity. I learnt to ignore his moods, his disappearances and his fury as he blamed me for his infidelity. I can't tell you the number of furious partners I've had to deal with when they've come knocking to find Stanley…the man is an immoral shit with no thought for anyone else except himself. All that matters to Stanley, is Stanley. Even now when he should be taking life easy, he's constantly on the internet chasing young women, I don't know what he thinks is going to happen…who would have sex with that?'

I laugh out loud at her final comment, she's such a lovely woman who doesn't deserve a minute of what Stanley has put her through. I apologise to her again and explain that when he contacted me on the dating site he used a picture of himself as a young man and I also told her that he had told me she was dead and they had no children. I felt awful telling her but she didn't bat an eyelid, she had heard it all before;

'The reason I've come to see you today Ann is firstly to apologise for my husband's behaviour. I bet your face was a picture when he arrived on your date! I'm guessing your shock was soon replaced with sympathy because you thought he was a sweet and frail old man who had nobody in the world, until he started leering over you, then you must have wondered what the hell was going on. Secondly I wanted to say to you, live your life Ann. Don't let anyone put you down, I should have left years ago but I felt keeping my family together was more important than how I felt. I sacrificed my own happiness when I didn't need to. My boys would have been fine without Stanley, it wasn't like he was a hands on father in the first place. I've been with Stanley so long I suppose I had a form of Stockholm syndrome, I knew he wasn't right and I deserved better. But love had been replaced by familiarity and I couldn't imagine what I would do without him. It took me forty years to finally realise my life would be so much better without him. Do what makes you happy Ann and never let any cunt piss on your bonfire, you're only here once and you need to make every minute count!'

I feel nothing but admiration for Doreen, she's a wonderful woman and swears like a trooper…she's fabulous and clearly knows Stanley very well as I couldn't have described our date better myself. How many women had that man had? Doreen doesn't say but reading between the lines I'm guessing his little black book was bulging at the seams. I almost pity Stanley for not realising what he had, wasting his life chasing something better when he could never find anyone better than the woman he had at home;

'So what are you going to do Doreen? Are you having to nurse Stanley back to health?'

'Fuck that darling, I've wasted too much time on that nasty piece of work. I'm seventy years old and finally I'm going to start living my best life. Yesterday, I emptied our joint bank account and tomorrow I'm off on a round the world cruise. I'm so excited, I haven't been abroad for years. I'm going to see the world, I'm going to savour every second and you never know I might meet my Mr Perfect, Lord knows I could do with a good seeing too, Stanley hasn't been able to get a hard on for years.'

With that, I spit my coffee out again, I hope I'm just like Doreen when I grow old. She's fun, sparkling and deserves the best. I hope she meets her Mr Perfect, better still if he's twenty years younger…fuck you Stanley your wife deserves so much better! I wonder what he'll think when he finds out she's going? I don't think he's going to be very happy losing control after all these years;

'So what do you think Stanley will say when you tell him you're going?'

'Ann, I couldn't give two flying shits what he thinks. He's got enough food to last him in the freezer and I've okayed it with his Doctor. Our next door neighbour is going to pop in to check on him every day which will be hilarious because he absolutely detests her. She's a big talker and he finds everything that comes out of her mouth irrelevant, so of course I had to tell her he might be lonely and in need of a good long chat. I've wasted forty years of my life on that man and I don't intend to waste another minute.'

She really is inspirational, I get up and give her a big hug, she's freed herself from her shackles and I have nothing but admiration for her. We chat for a bit longer before we finish our coffee and she promises to keep in touch. I do hope she does, I would love to know what happens on her cruise. We say our goodbyes and just as Doreen is leaving she turns back;

'Remember Ann, you only get one shot at life so be happy.'

I sit back and reflect on the conversation we've just had, Doreen is right in everything she's saying. As much as I admire her, I don't want to get to seventy and feel like I've wasted a moment of my life, I don't want to have any regrets or think 'what if'. So I really need to go for it with Ryan. I can succeed in my quest for sexual liberation, I can be an erotic goddess, but maybe a bit of romance as well wouldn't be a bad thing.

CHAPTER EIGHT

Ryan (again)

I just got back from my coffee with Doreen when Ryan called. I think he must be interested, he called me as soon as his art class finished. After a couple of days messaging and chatting over the phone we are meeting up tonight. He has VIP tickets for a new wine bar in town and I'm his plus one...check me out, I'm a VIP now. Finally I can actually get dressed up to the nines, I feel like I've been wearing nothing but jeans recently. I'm going for a long silver cocktail dress which is split up to the thigh and in the best tradition of erotic goddesses, I've bought myself a pair of six inch patent leather stilettos. As you may remember, I have tried and failed in high heeled shoes before and these fuckers are even higher so today, I am going to take my own advice and I am mainly going to be learning to walk in them. I get them out of the box and fuck, they are high! They slip on easily and actually feel quite comfortable, standing up is a challenge and I wobble slightly until I manage to get my balance. I do a few circuits of the house, go up and down the stairs a couple of times and you know what, I think I've got it! If my 'fuck me' shoes don't get me a shag tonight I think may as well give up!

I've spent the rest of the afternoon getting ready, I've done the obligatory muff trim, sorted out my unruly armpits and now I'm waiting for Ryan to arrive. I'm wearing my hair up for a change. I think an 'up do' suits a cocktail dress. Ha, listen to me, who the fuck do I think I am…stylist to the stars? I hear a car pull up outside and forget I'm wearing skyscraper heels as I rush out of the front door, I wobble and it feels like I'm going over but somehow, by some miracle I manage to regain my balance without anybody noticing (note to self…do not under any circumstances run in these shoes). I get into the taxi and Ryan looks edible in his black suit, think James Bond but better looking and more charming. He kisses me on the cheek and immediately takes hold of my hand, my fanny starts to tingle…something tells me she's going to get a damn good seeing to later on.

I feel like I'm at the Oscars, we step out of the taxi and walk down a red carpet to get in, the local press are taking photographs and I actually feel quite important. There's a waiter standing at the entrance handing out complimentary glasses of champagne…I don't mind if I do. The wine bar itself is festooned with balloons and twinkly lights…suddenly my imagination takes me to my wedding reception, Ryan sweeps me up in his arms as we are about to do the first dance…I just can't help myself can I? I'm brought back down to earth when Ryan asks if I'd like a glass or bottle of Prosecco? I've already got champagne and I need to keep my wits about me tonight so opt for just a glass. I find a table as he waits at the bar, I don't think I ever seen so many glamorous women in one place at the same time. I do find them slightly intimidating, I feel like I'm back in the changing rooms at school again, slightly inadequate and lacking in the chest department. The bar is awash with sequins and fake tits and the smell of fake tan hangs heavily in the air. Clearly on the prowl (bitches...) they start to encircle Ryan at the bar, they are hunting him down like a pack of hyenas. I watch him carefully, I'm intrigued as to what he's going to do. They are almost on top of him now trout pouting as if their lives depended on it, one woman is literally trying to thrust her more than ample bosom in his face. Ryan isn't fazed by them at all. To my absolute delight, he gently moves them out of the way, walks purposefully to our table and kisses me on the lips…take that slags!

Our table is right next to the dance floor and every opportunity I get, I slip my shoes off to let my poor feet recover. Ryan is such good company, I haven't laughed so much in ages. He keeps dragging me onto the dance floor which is a bit tricky as I have to put my shoes back on each time. He's a very good mover, we've danced quickly, we've danced slowly...I swear he thinks he's on Strictly Come Dancing! Every time we hit the dance floor I feel the hyenas watching, but Ryan only has eyes for me. I love that they can't understand why he isn't giving them a second glance....he's with me and he's happy, he clearly likes my natural breasts and my lumps and bumps (as he puts it) make me real. I've had a wonderful evening, we've laughed, danced and kissed all night long and he made a point of introducing me to his friends, which is a good sign isn't it? Neither of us want the night to end so we go back to his. When we arrive we head straight for the living room and Ryan pours us both a large brandy. I notice that the picture he drew of me has been framed and takes pride of place over the fire place. He sees me looking at it;

'It took everything I had to stay professional whilst I drew you, I wanted you so badly.'

Fucking hell, did he really just say what I thought he just said? Is this another dream? I surreptitiously pinch myself, it hurts...I'm not dreaming! He stands up and I walk towards him like the erotic goddess I know I can be. He takes me in my arms and kisses me, he expertly unzips my dress and it falls to the floor. Next he undoes my bra and flings it across the room. He picks up his glass of brandy, drips it across my breasts and licks it off as he plays with my nipples. His hand reaches into my knickers, he expertly parts my lips with his fingers and teases my clit. I'm wet and judging by what I've just felt in his trousers, he's ready to explode. I unzip him, drop to my knees and start to suck his cock, he groans and gently pulls my hair. Ryan tells me to stop, he wants to fuck me…finally I'm going to get a decent shag. He pulls off his trousers, I throw off my knickers and I'm just about to take off my shoes when he says;

'No Ann, keep the shoes on, they're sexy as hell!'

Whatever turns him on…I knew the shoes were a good idea! He's sitting on the settee his huge erection waiting for me. I step towards him, I'm completely naked apart from my shoes, I'm living my erotic dream! Look at me posh bird from 50 Shades of Grey, this is how you do it! I suck my stomach in and walk seductively towards him. His arms are outstretched, his cock is beckoning me and I'm just about there when my ankle goes…stupid fucking shoes! I feel myself falling, everything happens in slow motion, I hit my head on a side table and then nothing…until;

'Hello Ann, Ann, can you hear me my name is Mark I'm a paramedic.'

He's a para what now? I feel woozy and my head hurts;

'We're going to take you to hospital Ann, you've had nasty bang to the head and I think we need to get a Doctor to take a look at you.'

Thankfully Ryan covered me with a throw before the paramedics arrived and now he retrieves my knickers from behind the settee and gives me one of his shirts to put on so I don't feel so exposed. He insists on coming to the hospital with me and holds my hand in the ambulance. I think this one is definitely a keeper.

'I'm so sorry Ryan, it was such a lovely evening and I've ruined it.' I feel like crying, until…

'You've ruined nothing, there'll be other evenings…if you want?'

If I want, are you joking of course I want. I squeeze his hand tighter and my fanny would be tingling if my head wasn't throbbing so much. We arrive at the hospital and the ambulance crew wheel me in. I can't believe my luck, Little Miss Smug Bitch isn't on reception and the lady who books me in is absolutely lovely. I'm taken through to a cubicle and

I don't care how long I have to wait, Ryan is with me and I feel blissfully happy. A nurse pops her head around the curtain and tells me it won't be too long before a Doctor comes to see me. So that means it won't be long until I'm sandwiched between the lovely Ryan and Dr Gorgeous. The bump on my head although painful and unattractive may actually have been worth it!

I send Ryan off to get himself a coffee, it's been a long night and he's starting to look a bit tired. Within seconds of him leaving the nurse pops her head around the cubicle and tells me the Doctor is on their way. I brace myself for Dr Gorgeous and since it's just going to be me and him, I unbutton the shirt I'm wearing so I show a little cleavage and as I'm still wearing those stupid fucking shoes I decide to use them to my advantage. I throw off the sheet that's covering me and cross my legs seductively…I'm waiting Dr G. As the curtain to my cubicle is slowly being drawn back I feel butterflies in my stomach, I smile seductively until I see the Doctor. To my horror, it's not Dr Gorgeous it's…Sylvia, Josh's mother! Fuck, I had no idea she was a Doctor! How the hell is that woman a Doctor? She's got the bedside manner of a serial killer! She's just standing there starting at me, her piercing eyes narrow and flicker of recognition crosses her face. I see her staring at my shoes and I'm sure she mouths 'slut'. Feeling a little too exposed I quickly cover myself with the sheet...I'm clearly being punished for being disloyal to Ryan. But let's face it taking into account my past dating history, I can't really be blamed for keeping all my options open. Sylvia's mouth twitches as she's about to speak;

'I've read your notes, I see you fell...I'm not surprised wearing shoes like that.'

She's as cold as I remember her and in a panic I say the first thing that comes into my head;

'How's Josh, has he left home yet?'

Her breathing starts to get heavier, I've obviously pissed her off;

'Joshua is fine thank you. He's seeing a lovely girl, she's friend of the family so I know exactly where she's been. They are very happy, so don't you even think about contacting him again...ever!'

Poor Josh, he's royally fucked with Sylvia for a Mother, I just hope one day he grows the balls to walk out of the door and never go back. As for his poor girlfriend, I wish her all the luck in the world...she's going to need it. I decide not to say anything else and feel distinctly uncomfortable as Sylvia checks my eyes, I'm face to face with my nemesis and I feel like she's looking into my soul. She quickly scribbles something in my notes, tells me the nurse will give me a leaflet on head injuries and discharges me. Just as she turns to leave Ryan gets back with his drink, she looks at him menacingly and as she passes him whispers through gritted teeth;

'Is she with you? Be careful, she's a slut.'

Ryan is furious and is about to challenge her when I tell him not to bother, I explain that I went on a date with a guy who had the most frightening, over bearing Mother I had ever met. The date was a disaster culminating in me making a rapid escaped from a raging Sylvia who wasn't prepared to share her son with anyone. He laughs and tells me I haven't had much luck...he doesn't know the fucking half of it! I grab the head injury leaflet from the nurse and leave the hospital as quickly as I can. I'm a little disappointed that I didn't get to see Dr Gorgeous, but Ryan more than make up for it. He takes me back to mine where he tucks me up in bed and is more than happy to oblige when I ask him to join me. Neither of us are feeling particularly like doing anything other than sleep, so that's what we do. I spend the rest of the night and most of the morning asleep in Ryan's arms. I think

I have finally done it, I've found my Mr Romance and my Mr Uninhibited rolled into one. I feel happy and content and I'm going to enjoy the moment as long as it lasts.

CHAPTER NINE

More lessons learnt

I haven't been around much the past few weeks, I've been spending more and more time at Ryan's. I'm loved up, happy and pleased to say my sex drought finally came to an end a couple of nights after I hurt my head. Ryan had popped over to mine with a chocolate hamper…yes he is fucking perfect. He blamed himself for me falling over, he felt that if he hadn't of asked me to keep my shoes on it wouldn't have happened. He's quite right but I won't hold it against him! I wasn't expecting him when he arrived and answered the door wearing nothing but towel as I had just had a bath. Naturally I was delighted to see him and even more delighted with the chocolate! He stepped into the house and shut the door behind him. As he reached down to kiss me my towel fell down, I didn't make any attempt to hide my nakedness, this was my one shot as getting a shag and I was going to take it. I took the chocolate hamper out of his hands and unceremoniously threw it into the living room. Then I pulled him down to the floor, unzipped his trousers and he fucked me there and then. No props, no erotic tricks just a good old fashioned shag. It didn't last long and there was no earth shattering orgasm but it was lovely and it was a start. I'm also pleased to report there were no pints of Guinness involved in any way whatsoever!

So what else have I learnt from my latest (and hopefully last) attempts at online dating. Firstly and this is quite important. If you ever keep a souvenir from a date, hide it somewhere nobody will ever find it...not in the tea towel drawer in your kitchen. If it hadn't have been Tom who had found it, it could have been my Mother and that would have involved a whole new level of explaining myself. Maybe it was for the best that Tom found Daniel's wax bellend. Firstly, said bellend is now destroyed and I won't ever have to worry about anyone finding it again and secondly, if Tom hadn't of dumped me I would never have met Ryan. Tom was lovely but I don't think it would have lasted, I think I'm much better suited to Ryan...he's definitely 'the one'. I know I said Tom was 'the one' but a lady is entitled to change her mind isn't she? Next, love balls are an interesting idea. To be honest they didn't do all that much for me, once I got it into my head that my fanny sounded like a walking wind chime I just didn't feel it. Whatever you do, and I can't stress this enough always read the instructions. Why the fuck did I not read the instructions and how stupid was I to actually think it was a good idea to insert the string as well? Just spending two minutes reading the instructions would have saved me the humiliation of having to have them manually removed, if it wasn't for the fact I got to see Dr Gorgeous it would have been a total disaster.

Never trust a man who uses a black and white photograph on his dating profile, okay, maybe that's taking it a bit far as some people do prefer black and white pictures, but be wary. I thought Stanley was an enigmatic, arty type using a black and white photo for dramatic effect...he was a fucking pensioner! I thought I was doing my bit for the community by spending the evening with him, I thought he was a sweet, lonely old man when in reality he was a lecherous, dick pic sending philanderer...so never judge a book by its cover. All men are capable of lying, when Stanley should have been spending the autumn years of his life with his loyal and long suffering wife, he was prowling dating sites looking for a younger model...twat. What have I learnt from pretending Stanley was my Dad in order to spend time with Daniel...absolutely nothing. I hold my hands up, it was wicked and I am most likely going to hell, but it did mean I got to spend little bit of time with the delectable Daniel. Give me a break, I was mourning the loss of his wax bellend and spending a bit of time with him gave me closure.

The countryside is a very dangerous place! Not only is it an empty wilderness, there are cows everywhere. They are wandering around like they own the place, shitting where they feel like and if they get close to you they will try and eat you...that may sound over dramatic but I'd love to know how you'd feel if you woke up to a cow happily licking your ear lobe. Which leads me to never trust a man who loves the countryside, one minute he's romancing you with a fancy picnic, the next he's driving down a remote country lane so you can join the local dogging club. No fucking way, the cheeky bastard, what made him think I'd want to have sex with random strangers? He could have asked me, given me a choice but he so arrogant to think I was just going to go for it. What did he expect me to say?

'Oh Andrew, thank you so much for giving me the opportunity to have sex with Kev, Bob and Trev from the Farmer's Arms. I've never seen them before in my life but I'm more than happy to open my legs for them.'

'A mask, thank you so much! I always wanted to hide my face whilst having sex with strangers.'

'Dogging how charming, of course I'll give it a go.'

Cheeky twat! I didn't really understand it to be honest, Andrew was good looking, intelligent, funny...he could have had anyone he wanted, but preferred anonymous group sex. If you're on a date in the heart of the countryside and the man you are with suddenly hands you a mask…run a mile.

Roller skating is fun! Never let demons from your past stop you do anything. I was wary of going to the Roller Disco because it brought back memories of Julie Rigby and the cool girls at school, but I did it, I enjoyed it and I was actually quite good at it. I may not have had pink laces but I rocked the rink! Never have a bath in a hurry and leave the house with water in your ear, temporary deafness can cause all sorts of misunderstandings and you may end up getting a lifetime ban from your local Chinese restaurant. I've replayed that conversation with Ethan in my head a hundred times and although I struggled to hear what he was saying I was completely oblivious to some of the terminology he was using, I definitely need to have another look at the Urban Dictionary at some point. Don't be fooled by a sweet, nerdy man. Ethan looked like butter wouldn't melt in his mouth and I really thought that despite the fact I towered over him we got on well. But no, he sacked me off, thought I was nothing more than friend material. When push came to shove he just wasn't prepared to give me a chance. Would I have let him bash my back doors in? A lady never tells, so you'll just have to keep wondering about that one.

Don't live in the past. I fucked up with Daniel, I fucked up with his wax bellend and I should have accepted it was never going to happen and moved on. But I clung on to the hope that one day we would be reunited and I could continue my erotic adventure with him...for fucks sake, I only met him once, I really don't know why he impacted me so much. Anyway, it was never going to happen, he was just being polite in the pub when Stanley had his heart attack, doing what any good friend would. The dream I had was amazing and at least now I know what a Hollywood Wax is, but it showed me that it was unhealthy to keep chasing the impossible. It was time to let go of the Daniel fantasy, whilst I was still longing for a second chance, no one was going to be able to compete and I was stopping myself from being happy. Miss Fucking Perfection Personified was obviously his new girlfriend and there was no way I could compete with her. Daniel called me to see how my imaginary Dad was, but that was it. He wasn't going to call again, he had moved on. I was just a distant, probably quite bad memory to him and there was never going to be a repeat performance, even if I did promise to get rid of all the candles in my house. Daniel was an experience, part of life's rich tapestry. I didn't really know him and you now what, I bet he wasn't all that perfect...nobody is.

Never do anything you don't want to, I hate horror films but to impress Ryan I didn't tell him. If I'm honest the film was shit, cheesy shlock horror with no story or direction, but that's what some people love about horror movies. If I'd been straight up with Ryan I would have saved myself the embarrassment of nearly fainting at the sight of fake blood and the couple behind us would have been saved from being showered in popcorn. That said, if I hadn't of nearly fainted, he wouldn't have taken me home and we might not be where we are today. I found being drawn naked totally empowering, I was living my best erotic life and have been immortalised in pencil. It could be a bit awkward when I finally get to meet his parents, can you imagine we'll be drinking tea and making small talk in the shadow of my tits and muff. Maybe I'll ask him to take it down when I meet them. If something seems good, don't be too suspicious. It's just possible that everything is above board. Spying on Ryan and ending up face first in a bush was a bit of a low point, but like I said at the time it was only to be expected that I was going to be suspicious. All my dates prior to this had been such a disaster I was guilty of assuming Ryan was messing me around.

Doreen...what a woman! She's living proof that it's never too late. She's been in touch since she went on her cruise, apparently Stanley was furious but she stood her ground and currently she's somewhere in the Atlantic Ocean making up for all those lost years. Forty years she put up with Stanley's infidelity, forty years of not being cherished and yes she should have left sooner, but she's going to make up for it now. I'm definitely going to take her advice on board and do what makes me happy. Why should I conform to other people's ideas of what I should and shouldn't do…I've tried conforming to the rules of erotica and look where that's got me! For now Ryan is making me happy and I'm going to enjoy ever minute of it. Meeting Doreen was an education, who knew old ladies swore so much, I don't know why but I always imagined that by the time you turned fifty a swearing filter switched on and you would never utter and expletive again.

Shoes….fucking shoes! I knew I struggled to walk in three inch stilettos, so what the fuck possessed me to go for six inches? I mean they did look good and they turned Ryan on, but they were a danger to my health. Looking back I can see it was never going to end well, I'm naturally clumsy and should just stick to flats. Although I did manage to do the whole evening without falling over, the fact they let me down when I was within a cock's length of getting a shag made me hate them, so as soon as Ryan left the next day I bid the shoes a not so fond farewell and threw them in the bin. I need to go with what I'm comfortable with, not what I think makes me an erotic goddess. I'm sure if I greeted Ryan completely naked apart from my pink trainers he would find that erotic. I think I've come to the conclusion that erotica is what you make it and not what the books tell you. Finally...Dr Gorgeous. I'm with Ryan now so I really need to get Dr Gorgeous out of my head. I know nothing about him apart from he is actually gorgeous with a smile to die for. He has a lovely bedside manner and always manages to put me at ease no matter what predicament I've got myself into. But now I know Sylvia is lurking around the hospital I am going to do everything I can to avoid it, which means I probably won't see Dr Gorgeous again...he might be happily married for all I know, so I think now is a good time to put that particular fantasy to bed.

So where does that leave me? After more dating disasters than I'd care to remember, I'm blissfully happy with Ryan, we've only been together for a few weeks but so far things are looking wonderful. He's kind, thoughtful and has a brilliant personality, it's a huge bonus that he's also incredibly good looking and is he good in bed? That's for me to know and you to never to find out! My membership of the dating site has been cancelled, hopefully for good this time and my Ann Summers Rep hasn't heard from me for ages, her dildo sales must be well down! I've deleted Daniel's number from my phone and I'm more than ready to move on. I know nothing in life is certain, but I think I finally have my happy ending. Keep your fingers crossed!

If you haven't read the first book in the 'Wax and Whips' series ('Wax Whips and my Hairy Bits') here's the first few pages...

Wax Whips and My Hairy Bits...

CHAPTER ONE

Me

I used to love reading romance novels, nothing modern, just good old fashioned Victorian romantic literature. It was a time of innocence, the pace of life was slower, the men more charming. A time where you didn't have to conform to female stereotypes online, where you never needed to ask 'does my arse look big in this' because everyone looked big in a bustle and no fucker was going to get a look at your arse until you had a ring on your finger. It gave me hope that there was a Mr Romance out there for us all and then suddenly it dawned on me that actually it was all a little bit dull. It took me a bit of time to realise where it was all going wrong, but then it became clear. These novels, lovely as they were, were missing one vital component...they didn't do cock.

My name is Ann, not regal Anne, just plain, boring, unexciting Ann. I often wonder how my life would have turned out if my parents had just given me that extra 'e'. I am thirty-two years old, no spring chicken and no stranger to the dating scene. I work in marketing which isn't as glamorous as it sounds and if I'm honest it bores the shit out of me. The search for my Mr Romance had led me to a succession of short, infuriating relationships where the sex had been no more exciting than a blow job and a quick shag (missionary position). I needed less Mr Romance and more Mr Uninhibited. I needed excitement, hot wax and a fucking good seeing to. I was single, more than ready to mingle and had read a shit load of Erotica so I knew exactly what I had to do in order to embark on a new sexual adventure. I wanted no strings sex, none of that emotional bollocks, just a good hard fuck and maybe a cup of coffee in the morning. I'm bored of feeling boring. I don't want to be Ann who's a good laugh, I want to be Ann who's amazing in bed, I want to be the shag that stays with you a lifetime, never bettered or forgotten.

My longest relationship had lasted nearly two years, Hayden. We met when we were both at university. I was so young and inexperienced I didn't really know what a good shag was. I lost my virginity to him after four bottles of Diamond White and maybe it was because I was pissed, or maybe because he was shit at shagging, but it was a completely underwhelming experience. There was no earth shaking orgasm, just the feeling something was missing and a sore fanny for a couple of days. We muddled along, foreplay was always the same, I gave him a blow job, he tried to find my clitoris...the man needed a fucking map. Sex was nearly always missionary, I'd sneak on top whenever I could, but he'd always flip me over for a quick finish. Maybe we just became too familiar with each other but when he started to not take his socks off when we had a shag I knew it was time to move on. He wasn't that arsed to be honest, I think he'd started to prefer his games console to me anyway and if he could have stuck his knob in it I'm sure he would have dumped me before I dumped him. My relationship history since Hayden has been unremarkable, hence my decision to ditch the romance novels and dive head long, or should that be muff long, into Erotica.

I'm suppose you could say I'm reasonably pretty and my face is holding up well, which is surprising given my twenty a day smoking habit, absolute love of kebabs and a probable dependency on Prosecco. My tits aren't too bad, they measure in at a 36C and I'm pleased to say they are still nice and perky and probably a few years off resembling a Spaniel's ears. My legs are long and shapely and the cellulite on my arse can be hidden with a good, supportive pair of knickers. Thongs just aren't going to happen, sorry Erotica but negotiating with a piece of cheese wire up my arse does not do it for me whatsoever. I've been researching my subject well recently, and one of the first rules when embarking on an erotic adventure seems to be that one must have a shaven haven, a freshly mown lawn, a smooth muff...I think you get the picture. I need to think carefully about how I am going to achieve my erotica ready fanny as the expression 'bearded clam' doesn't describe the half of it!

I don't fancy having my fanny flaps waxed and shaving isn't really an option as I'm petrified I'll get a shaving rash. So the only option I've got is hair remover cream. A quick trip to the shops and it's mission accomplished; my lady garden is smothered in intimate hair remover cream. It looks like a Mr Whippy with sprinkles but definitely no chocolate flake. It's not the most attractive look in the world, I'm staggering around like a saddle sore old cowboy, but it's going to be worth it...I am Ann without an 'e' and without pubes, a bald fannied paragon of sexual liberation. That bird with the posh name in 50 shades of whatever is going to have nothing on me! Though I have to admit, the undercarriage was a bit of a nightmare and to be honest it does sting a bit. At least I don't have to wait too long and then I will be smooth, shiny and....ouch...I'm fucking burning now!

Burning is not right surely? Jesus, my flaps are on fire. Give me a minute I need to jump in the shower and get this shit off.

I just spent four fucking hours in A&E. I washed the cream off and my minge was glowing red and burning like a bastard which was almost bearable until the swelling started. I could feel my lips starting to throb, they were pulsating like a rare steak. I didn't want to look down, but I knew I had to…fuck me I had testicles, just call me Johnny Big Bollocks because that is what I had. I quickly checked Dr Google and the best thing for swelling is elevation and an ice pack, so I spent the best part of half an hour with my minge in the air and a packet of frozen peas clamped between my thighs. Needless to say it had no effect at all and it became painfully clear that I was going to have to haul my now damp, swollen crotch to the hospital. Never before have I felt so humiliated, having to describe in intimate detail my problem to little Miss Smug Bitch at reception;

'So, you've come to A&E today because your vagina is swollen'...

…well it's my vulva actually but let's not split pubic hairs, or try and get them off with cunting hair remover cream. Sour face huffed and puffed and eventually booked me in, I spent what felt like an eternity pacing around...I couldn't sit down, my testicles wouldn't allow it and by this time a ball bra wouldn't have gone amiss. The Doctor I saw, who was absolutely gorgeous (the one time I didn't want to show an attractive man my fanny) and, when he wasn't stifling a laugh, couldn't have been more sympathetic. I'd had an allergic reaction and he'd prescribe me some anti-histamines which would bring the swelling down, my labia would return to their normal size and other than some skin sensitivity for a few days I would be fine but under no circumstances was I to use hair remover cream again as next time the reaction could be even worse. Though what could be worse than the whopping set of bollocks I'd grown I don't know. So that's that, I'm going to have to go au natural. Which is fine by me, I'd rather have a hairy beaver than an angry one.

A few hours later and my muff has more or less returned to normal and other than feeling slightly itchy seems to be perfectly fine. I've crossed shaven haven off my to do list and need to carry on with my preparation. As you may have already gathered, I've got a lot of work to do. I've noticed in most of the Erotica I've read that the words penis and vagina are rarely used, so I need to practise my sexual vocabulary, I need to learn how to talk dirty...I need to do my Erotica homework. I've had another flick through some of my books and there's no way I can call my vagina 'my sex' I know strictly speaking it is, but for fuck's sake…'my sex craves you', 'my sex needs your sex' it's all sounds a bit contrived if you ask me so I think I'll check out the Urban Dictionary.

I've just spent a good hour trawling through and my God what an education that was. Either I'm more wet behind the ears than I thought I was or some of the things I've just read are made up, check out 'Angry Pirate'…that's not for real, is it? I'm ready to try some of the new words and phrases I've learnt. I need to be all pouty lipped and doe eyed as I look in the mirror, moisten my lips and purr:

'I want to suck your length'

'Do you want to drink out of my cream bucket'

'My clit is hard and ready to be licked'

'My vagina is the most magical place in the world, come inside'

What the fuck was I thinking, I can't say this shit! Firstly the doe eyed, pouty lip thing makes me look like I'm pissed and secondly I can't do this without laughing. I'm much more comfortable with 'do you fancy a pint of Guinness and a quick shag'. I quickly give my head a wobble, comfortable is boring. I'm in this for the excitement and the clit tingling thrill (see I did learn something). Maybe I'll just opt for quiet and mysterious, let my body do the talking and my mouth do the sucking (I'm really starting to get this now). So that's the plan, my persona will be a sultry erotic goddess who doesn't say much, I'll be irresistible, a fabulous shag who doesn't want a conversation, no chat just sex.

The last part of my preparation is what on earth am I going to wear? If I'm going for the mysterious look does that mean I'm going to have to channel my inner sex goddess, or does it mean I go for a prim and proper, hair up, professional look? Maybe a combination of both, tight fitting dress, hair up and glasses, then I can do the whole taking my glasses off and flicking my hair down thing. The hair flicking thing however is a bit of an issue for me: my hair is naturally curly...really curly, at university my nickname was 'pube head' which probably tells you all you need to know, so I'm going to have to straighten it to within an inch of its life. From frump to fox...check me out. Today is going to be an exciting day. I'm just waiting for the postman to arrive, I've ordered some proper lingerie. I've gone for two sets initially, traditional black and racy red. Shit, should I have ordered a dildo? I forgot about a fucking dildo and candles, I forgot candles! What about a butt plug...what actually is a butt plug? I can't be erotic if I'm not dripping hot wax on him whilst pleasuring myself with a multi speed vibrating dildo…okay, so maybe not at the same time but you get my drift. Handcuffs! Shit, I'm not very good at this, he'll just have to tie me up with my big knickers.

The postman came, and I swear he had a knowing glint in his eye when he asked me to sign for my delivery or maybe he just read the label on the back of the parcel, cheeky bastard. It took me a while to build up the courage but here I am, standing in front of a full length mirror wearing a bright red, lacy push up bra, matching arse covering comfortable pants, a suspender belt and black stockings. I'm not sure. My tits are standing to attention and look like boiled eggs in a frilly egg cup, they are virtually dangling from my ear lobes and I swear you can see my minge stubble. So the new plan will be to go for subdued or even better, no lighting at all. I think it's all starting to look really erotic… bushy fanny, no filthy talking and everything done in the dark. The scene is set and I'm ready to get out there. No strings, erotic sex here I come. Well, not quite, I need to sign up to a dating site.

I take a selfie of myself looking as sultry as possible (not doe eyed or pouty, we know that doesn't work) I decide to show a little bit of cleavage and a little bit of leg, but not too much I want to leave my potential dates gagging to see more…I'm such a temptress. I've written and rewritten my profile about twenty times, it has to be just right and I think on my twenty first attempt I've finally done it:

'Flirty thirty two year old,

I work in marketing,

I like to get my head down in both the boardroom and the bedroom,

I'm looking for no strings attached fun,

Hobbies include reading, cooking and amateur dramatics.'

I know, you don't have to tell me, it's painfully shit. Hopefully they'll just look at my profile picture and to be honest at this point I don't care, I've submitted everything and I am now a fully paid up member of a dating site.

It takes a couple of hours for my phone to eventually ping with a notification that I have a message, I'm trembling with excitement as I open it…

'You've got nice tits'

Fuck me, 'You've got nice tits' is that it? I mean it's nice he thinks I've got nice tits, but I was expecting a little bit more. No, hang on he's sent a picture...it's a dick! He's sent me a picture of his dick, eww I don't think I've ever seen such a stumpy little penis, it's got a hugely bulbous bellend which looks like it's going to explode at any minute and hang on, it looks like it's winking at me...I'm never going to be able to unsee that! I quickly delete the message, when my phone pings again...It's another dick, not the same dick, this one is long, thin and veiny as fuck. Maybe I'm being too fussy, knobs aren't supposed to be attractive are they? My phone is quickly becoming a rogues gallery of ugly shlongs. I'm really starting to think maybe this wasn't a good idea, I know I said I wanted plenty of cock, but this wasn't exactly what I meant. Three cocks later and just as I am about to give up on the whole idea (maybe a pint of Guinness and a quick shag isn't too bad after all) I get a message from Daniel. I check out his profile and he actually looks quite fit, he's good looking, athletic and he didn't send me a dick pic....

What happens next?...buy the book to find out!

Go to Amazon and search Wax Whips and My Hairy Bits S J Carmine

And...while I still I have you here I'd like to recommend a book of short stories from my talented brother, Richard Hennerley, that are full of love, magic, triumph, tragedy and whimsy...the book is called 'Floating Away' and here's part of one of the tales from the book...

The Boy who was Strange and Different

Part 1. Mother and Son.

Once upon a time... many, many years ago in a world long since forgotten, there was a country called Anywhere. And in the land of Anywhere there was a fine and prosperous city called Anyplace and in this fine city lived a woman who had three children, two girls and a boy.

Unfortunately for the children The Woman was a person of inordinate selfishness, one of those people who feel that they world revolves around them and them alone, someone who was prepared to do anything to get what she wanted. To make things worse, the children had lost their father at an early age. The poor man had died of a broken heart for during the course of his marriage to The Woman he had come to realise that she had not married him for love but simply as a way of escaping from her own background (which had been rather Poor And Mean) and gaining Financial Security and Social Standing. For his own reasons, which to this day remain unfathomable, the husband had loved The Woman dearly and simply could not reconcile the love he felt for her with the total lack of love she had for him.

So he succumbed to the Sadness Disease (which in your world you call cancer) but beat it to its fatal conclusion by drinking himself to death.

This left three children (another unfathomable that also remains unanswered to this day – exactly why did she have children?) to be raised by one very strange woman. The Woman only had two Real Loves and they were Social Standing and Gambling. She loved nothing more than praise and attention from friends, associates and The Neighbours and, in pursuit of such, would portray herself to those around her as a brave and valiant Single Mother who Devoted Her Life to raising and caring for her darling children, and such performance did indeed bring her much praise and her precious, desired Social Standing.

But The Woman's Truth as she presented it to the world was a Fiction. The Woman's children were left pretty much to bring up themselves, she was an Absent And Unconcerned parent for her love for herself and her needs was too great to spare any love for her children. She put food on the table and clothes on the children's backs but nothing else. And then not always, for almost every cent and penny that came into the household was spent on The Woman's other Great Love: gambling. Oh, how The Woman loved to gamble, for hours and days on end. She would gamble on horses, dogs, rabbits, flashing lights – anything that moved and presented a chance of a chance!

Growing up with this strange, self-obsessed woman was difficult for all three children but most particularly for The Boy. Girls are always cleverer about these things and The Boy's sisters had long since recognised The Mother for the Selfish And Uncaring creature she was and they had simply resolved to get on with life until such time as they were old enough to leave home and never come back. The Boy felt things more keenly for, like his father, he had, for yet another unfathomable reason to this day unexplained, a Deep And Abiding Love for his mother. And he desperately wanted her to return that love, to share a kind word, a warm embrace. Of course, The Woman never did any of these things but the more she showed The Boy that she had no love for him, the more he wanted her to love him and the harder he would try to be loved and he would say:

'Look at this, Mum',
'I love you, Mum',
'Look what we did at school today, Mum.'
'You look nice today, Mum.'
'I made this for you, Mum.'

And The Woman would grunt and turn her back on him and return to her gambling or telling stories to The Neighbours of her sacrifices for her children as a struggling Single Mother.

Truth be told, The Woman didn't just not love her son, she despised him. She saw him as a threat to her Social Standing for whilst The Boy had a pleasing and loving nature and was not unintelligent or untalented (indeed he had a beautiful singing voice) or unattractive, he was small for his fourteen years and had a certain gentle feyness about him – a degree of femininity that she disliked and distrusted. She was very concerned that the child might be a *falulah* (a 'falulah' is Anywhere slang that corresponds to words like 'queer' and 'faggot' in your world).

Now, this Tale is set in some years back in the history of Anywhere, before the brief Golden Age and social, cultural and economic blooming that occurred as a result of breaking the dead grip of The Greedy One Percent (sadly short-lived though that period was) and Social Attitudes were, particularly on matters of difference and sexuality, still very retarded – being identified as a falulah was a matter of great Social Embarrassment and shame and it was widely considered that a person was better off dead than falulah. So-

The Mother's suspicions that her son might be 'one of them' caused her considerable concern. Imagine the Social Shame of having a son who was inclined that way. What would the neighbours think? And the damage such shame would cause to her Social Standing! Unacceptable!

Then one day all The Woman's fears were confirmed for The Boy came back from school with a ripped shirt and a bloody lip and tears in his eyes. 'Mum,' he said, 'the other boys beat me and laughed at me and called me a falulah, why mum, why?'

And a spasm of pure terror and shame shot through The Woman. See, she had been right, the boy was a fulalah and now other people were beginning to notice! Oh, the shame, all those years of building up her Social Standing were going to be ruined by this horrible, useless falulah child.

'Well, I'm not surprised,' said the infuriated mother, 'I mean look at you, you're pathetic, you're so small, you're tiny compared to the other boys and you sound like a girl. Huh, they're right you are a falulah!' With these words she walked towards her child and The Boy, despite her harsh words, thought (or at least fervently hoped) that she was going to comfort him. Instead she stopped short of The Boy, raised a hand above her head and slammed it down with all her strength across his face, knocking him to the floor. 'Get upstairs to your room!' she screamed. And as the terrified child did just that, she screamed after him:

'Dwarf!'

'Midget!'

'Falulah!'

'Falulah!'

Calming herself, The Mother thought about what she should do. A falulah for a son, what a humiliation. She couldn't let this miserable child threaten her Social Standing – but short of murdering the child (which, to be quite frank, she would have done were it not for the fear of being caught) what could be done? And she thought. And she thought. And she thought. And she came up with a plan.

The next day, whilst The Boy was at school, she made her way to The Asylum For The Strange And The Different.

Part 2. The Asylum For The Strange And The Different.

To understand what happened next in this tale it is necessary to understand about The Asylum For The Strange And The Different and its position in Anywhere's society at this point in Anywhere's history. Fundamentally, it was a dumping ground – for The Strange and The Different – The Strange being those considered to be mad and The Different being those who didn't quite fit in with society because they perhaps had strange views and ideas, or whose politics were regarded as dangerous or who were, perhaps, falulahs.

Once an unfortunate individual was placed in The Asylum, that was it, They were gone. Lost. Invisible. Never to be heard from again. No inmates of The Asylum ever left that grim place alive.

And The Asylum was truly dreadful, a black pit of madness and despair: those who worked there only worked there as a very last resort, out of desperation to earn some kind of living. Faeries would not fly within a two mile radius of it and Trolls would not even mention it in conversation (to do so was considered to bring the worst of luck): even Death was a reluctant to go there, though The Devil did think it rather a fun place to visit. Certainly nobody ever came to see anybody at The Asylum; after all it was where Strange or Difficult were dumped and why, having got rid of them, would one want to visit them?

Within the walls of The Asylum there was no concept of treatment or care for its reluctant inmates. The Different were there simply to keep their disturbing ideas and proclivities away from wider society – that was all, nothing to do but keep them locked away until they died. The Different – they were just mad and there was nothing to done about that: in the land of Anywhere at this time madness was considered not be an illness or dysfunction but an Altered State. The belief was that mad people were mad because they had, in some way, communed with The Devil. During the course of their congress with Satan, he had allowed them to open the pages of his Book Of The Dead. The Devil's Book Of The Dead is a kind of Satanic Stamp Album. An album of huge size and length in which The Devil, the Ultimate Connoisseur Of Suffering, records (for his delight and delectation) the saddest of deaths – those being to The Devil (and to your narrator) the premature deaths, be it by disease or violence, of The Young And The Innocent. And each death is recorded not in words, instead it is written in emotion, in the pain and sadness that was endured in the course of that death. As such, The Devil's Book Of Death contains a depth of pain so great, so deep, so profound that to open even one page for one second is enough to plunge any man or woman into madness, a madness that is pure and unchangeable – an Altered State. All that is to be done with a person who has peered into The Devil's Book Of Death is to assign them until death to The Asylum For The Strange And The Different.

So, there you have it, The Asylum For The Strange And The Different was no more or no less than a place where those considered mad, different, awkward or embarrassing were sent to die. Once in, there was no way out except death. To be an inmate in The Asylum was to 'live' in a state of non-existence.

Let's return now to my little tale. Having been informed of the nature and purpose of The Asylum For The Strange And The Different you've probably guessed the purpose of The Mother's visit there. That's right, she'd gone there to visit the Director of The Asylum to plead her case for having The Boy admitted (dumped and forgotten until death) there. All in all, things went well for her. The Director, a miserable bigot of a man who abhorred difference of any kind and particularly falulahs, had agreed with her. Her case was justified, keeping a falulah in the family home would indeed result in Unacceptable Embarrassment to her with a concomitant drop in her Social Status. However, just to oil the wheels, smooth the path and get The Boy admitted the next day might she consider a Small Token Of Her Appreciation, maybe just lie back and lift up her skirt, just twenty minutes of her time?

The Mother considered the Director's request to have sex with her and thought, why not if it's going to get the job done and get that horrible child out my life? The decision was made all the easier to make because on the way to The Asylum she had suddenly realised another 'plus' of getting rid of The Boy: one less mouth to feed would mean more money for one of the true loves of her life – gambling! Don't be shocked, I did tell you she was a truly awful woman…

The next day, The Boy was getting ready for school (The Boy and his sister's always got themselves ready for school, The Mother never being awake that early in the day due to having been up late gambling) when, much to his surprise his mother appeared, fully dressed, bright and smiling.

'Well hullo, my little man!' she said cheerily, 'and how are you today? My son, my beloved son, you've been having a difficult time so today there'll be no school – you're coming to the shops with me and we're going to buy you a treat and then we'll go for a lovely Sludge burger!'

And The Boy beamed from ear to ear, for this was Heaven to him, at last his mother was being nice to him, the only thing he really, really wanted in life was finally coming to pass!

The Boy and his mother jumped into a clarb (the Anywhere equivalent of a London black cab) and began their journey. The Mother explained to The Boy that before they went to the shops she just had to stop off somewhere and 'pick something up for a friend.' The Boy nodded and smiled and took hold of his mother's hand and squeezed it gently. This vaguely repulsed The Mother but she accepted it, even squeezed The Boy's hand gently back – keep the horrible little thing happy and quiet, she thought, I'll soon be rid of it, she thought.

By and by, the clarb came to, you've guessed it, The Asylum For The Strange And The Difficult, and the mother said 'come on, little man, come with me – this thing I have to collect is quite heavy so you can give me a hand!'

Willingly The Boy jumped out of the clarb with his mother, happy to help. Seeing the huge, grey, bleak, hulking building before him he felt a sense of doom and despair but comforted himself with the thought that he was with his mother, she'd make sure that everything was fine.

Into The Asylum went mother and soon. Down long, depressing corridors painted that sickly, pale shade of green beloved by bureaucracies in all worlds everywhere, until they came to a blank, anonymous looking door. 'Ah, yes,' said the mother, 'this is where we should be – be a dear and pop into this room will you and pick up the package there…' and she swung open that anonymous door. And The Boy, eager to please, entered the room and before he could register the fact that it contained no package, two burly Asylum employees threw a thick, heavy net over him and wrestled him to the ground, dragging him out of the room and down, down, down another long, depressing corridor and as he kicked and screamed and was hauled away to a state of non-existence oh, how the mother laughed and she shouted:

'Idiot!'

'Midget!'

'Girl!'

'Falulah!'

'Falulah!'

And The Boy cried:

'Mummy!'

'No, mummy, no!'

'Why, mummy?'

'Why?'

'Why….'

What happens next? Buy the book (available in Kindle and paperback formats) and find out!

Go to Amazon and search RICHARD HENNERLEY
FLOATING AWAY

Printed in Great Britain
by Amazon